Mills & Boon
Best Seller Romance

A chance to read and collect some of the best-loved novels
from Mills & Boon—the world's largest publisher of romantic
fiction.

Every month, four titles by favourite Mills & Boon authors
will be re-published in the *Best Seller Romance series*.

A list of other titles in the *Best Seller Romance* series can be found
at the end of this book.

GW00706055

Margaret Rome

PALACE OF
THE HAWK

MILLS & BOON LIMITED
LONDON · TORONTO

First published 1974
Australian copyright 1981
Philippine copyright 1981
This edition 1981

© Margaret Rome 1974

ISBN 0 263 73493 5

Set in 11 on 12 pt. Linotype Baskerville

*Made and printed in Great Britain by
Richard Clay (The Chaucer Press) Ltd, Bungay, Suffolk*

CHAPTER ONE

LIKE a gnat contemplating an assault upon a sky-scraper, Lucille Lamb began ascending the gang-plank inclining upwards towards the towering bulk of ocean liner—thirteen storeys high, longer than three football fields. She wondered no longer why Shani had insisted so vehemently that if she had to endure the boredom of travelling to yet another god-forsaken spot chosen by her sadistically in-clined producer as the location for their next film, then the method of transportation must be left to her and the expense account to him! Grudgingly, Art Callahan had agreed. At the moment, Shani Sharon was the public's darling, sure-fire box office, which meant he could not afford to risk arousing the fiery petulance of the rising young star.

'Go right ahead, darling,' he had warily agreed, eyeing her passionate face with the disinterested aplomb of one who has seen many stars rise and fall, 'just so long as you remember you have a lead-ing man whose wishes are as important as your own.'

'Am I ever likely to forget *him*,' had been the scornful reply, 'when every breath you breathe forms his name? Tareq Hawke, the dynamic actor,' she mimicked sarcastically, 'the connoisseur of beau-tiful women!'

Lucille fumbled in her handbag and produced the required documents for scrutiny; tickets, pass-ports, visas, vaccination certificates, advance baggage receipts. 'Miss Sharon will be arriving on the boat train,' she explained absently, as she had done so many times before. 'I'd be grateful if you'd see to it that her embarkation is accomplished as quickly as possible before any possible autograph-hunters get wind of her presence.'

'Don't worry, Miss Lamb,' the amused officer sketched a salute as he handed back the papers, 'we're quite used to accommodating celebrities.'

She blushed, feeling slightly foolish. The mild rebuke was deserved—being so bound up in her job, so determined to allow Shani no cause for complaint, she had underestimated the efficiency that must obviously exist amongst the crew of the *Q.E. 2*, the vessel pronounced by many as the most notable ship in the world.

The attitude of the steward assigned to direct her to Shani's quarters was puzzling. Deferential to the point of obsequiousness, he projected silent awe along the length of the alleyways, then bowed almost reverently when finally they reached their destination and he flung open a door to allow her access into the suite. With a nod and a word of thanks Lucille stepped inside to feel immediately the cling of deep pile carpet around her ankles. Wide-eyed, she stared around at the luxury of her surroundings, wondering unbelievingly how even Shani had had the nerve to saddle her producer with the exorbitant expense such opulence was sure to entail.

Appropriately, a plaque on the door read 'Queen Anne Suite'. Inside, a lounge furnished in shades of gold made a perfect background for furniture relying upon effective use of figured walnut veneers so

6

characteristic of the tasteful period. Restrained elegance was the predominant theme, chairs and tables with gently curving forms lent an eighteenth-century elegance to a background of modern simplicity. Silverware with simple glowing surfaces complemented the character of the room, oblong slender-framed mirrors, graceful lamp-bases and a large drinks tray upon which was set a decanter and glasses sending out sparkles of pure crystal. A huge muslin-draped picture window held out a promise of superb views once the ship was under weigh and rising from one corner of the room was a curved staircase leading upwards to a second level where Lucille assumed she would find the bedroom. It was a delight almost impossible to believe, the blending of such delicate, old-world elegance into the confines of a bustling ship—and a sacrilege almost, to think of a Philistine such as Shani jarring the atmosphere with her supercilious image.

'You're sure this is Miss Sharon's suite?' she questioned the steward faintly.

'Oh, yes, miss,' he stressed with undoubted confidence. 'I've checked the reservations. The Queen Anne Suite is reserved for Miss Sharon and the Trafalgar Suite adjoining has been booked for a Monsieur Tareq Hawke.'

There was nothing she could do but accept it. Ructions were sure to ensue once Art Callahan arrived and realized the folly of allowing Shani her head, but nevertheless the luggage was waiting to be unpacked and piles of clothes would have to be pressed free of creases before the star's arrival.

With a resigned shrug, Lucille proceeded to carry out the task Shani had insisted no one else should

7

do, subduing her rising resentment with vocal reminders of the benefits to be gained from remaining in her job as secretary-companion to the
demanding young film star who preferred to forget,
except when it suited her, that the quiet girl who
moved silently in the background dealing calmly
and efficiently with a daily avalanche of jobs was
her cousin as well as an employee.

'No use moaning about Shani's selfishness,' she
lectured herself as she skimmed a small travelling
iron over delicate flounces. 'You've known about
her tantrums for years, but one of the reasons you
took the job was because you decided anything
could be tolerated for a chance to travel, remember? And you have travelled, my girl, practically
half way round the world these past two years, so
you can't say it hasn't all been worth while!'

A pensive, far-away look clouded eyes of solemn
grey. Had she dreamt those past experiences, or had
she really climbed the Spanish Steps in Rome,
delved the hearts of somnolent Portuguese villages,
learned to skin-dive in the warm waters off the
shores of Jamaica and even more exciting, tracked
wild game through African bush . . .

'Lucille, that dress cost the earth, *you fool*, can't
you smell burning . . . !'

'Dress?' For one infinitesimal second Lucille
faced her accuser with a look of vague puzzlement,
then a return with a look of vague puzzlement, then
a return to shocked reality drained her eyes of
dreams and her cheeks of softly flushed colour. 'Oh,
I'm so sorry, you startled me, Shani, I didn't hear
you come in . . . !' Swiftly she assessed the damage,
then with a nervous laugh tried to make amends.

8

'Luckily it's only a small singe on the inside of the hem. I'm sure I can repair it so you'll never know where it's been.'

With a furious twitch the dress was ripped from her hands and examined by its scandalized owner. Lucille studied her as she waited for her verdict, knowing full well that, slight or not, full capital was about to be made out of the mishap. Shani looked magnificent, a magnificence cultivated initially for the camera but which now had become so integral a part of her personality that she found it impossible to discard it even before an audience of one. Beautiful eyes swept wild green flame over the tainted dress and white teeth bit with theatrical anguish into a pink bottom lip trembling with petulance. As she bent to peer closer at the damage, hair the colour of polished chestnuts shimmered across her eyes and was swept back with impatient fingers made heavy by a clutch of costly rings. She drew herself up, her slender figure casting a shadow across Lucille's anxious face, and derided with the anger of one who refuses to be cheated out of an enjoyable scene.

'Are you seriously suggesting that *anything* you might do would make this dress wearable? It's ruined, *ruined*, and all because of sheer negligence!' Her breast rose and fell rapidly as she posed to act out a melodramatic finale. 'The cost of the dress will be deducted from your salary,' she decreed with hauteur, 'as a reminder to take more care of the property placed in your charge.'

Lucille's lips twitched, but she managed not to smile. She had received only one salary cheque in two years, as Shani well knew. Each time payment

9

had been due some mishap had occurred which had made it necessary for Shani to deduct the cost from Lucille's salary. This way, she had managed for two years to enjoy the services of a secretary-companion for the price of her keep and one month's pay. At first, Shani had been surprised at the ease with which this state of affairs had been accomplished, then surprise had turned to scorn when Lucille's reluctance to argue, her eagerness to keep her job, had become obvious—an eagerness Shani had begun exploiting to the full.

Warily she waited for Lucille's reaction, always expectant of reproach, but when Lucille showed acceptance with the meek request: 'Then may I keep the dress?' Shani's shrewd eyes glinted satisfaction.

Casually, she nodded; the disputed dress had been worn as often as was suitable for one so much in the public eye and both were aware that it had been due to be discarded. 'Very well,' she indulged the request regally. 'I'm not at all sure I ought to reward such negligence, but I've become so conditioned over the years to keeping you supplied with clothes that I now feel it's more of a duty. I can understand now how my parents must have felt when they were obliged to offer a home to an orphaned niece whose upbringing must surely have taxed an already over-strained budget.'

Familiar though she was with such cruel reminders, Lucille winced. Eyes of pained grey dominated delicate features made unconsciously patrician by an inbred dignity that forbade the momentary satisfaction of vulgar repartee. It was this air of breeding which had so often in the past influenced

Shani's spiteful digs, the only way she knew of assuaging the disquietening assessment of a solemn gaze which, though neither resentful nor condemning, had the power to make her feel decidedly uncomfortable.

'My parents could hardly have been expected to foresee sudden death so early in their lives,' Lucille choked on her humiliation. 'I'm certain that if they had, proper provision would have been made for my future. But in any case,' she continued with dignity, 'I was never at any time in my life made to feel a nuisance or a burden on your parents.'

Shani shifted uncomfortably, conscious of stirring jealousy. 'If you're referring to the many assurances you received from my mother and father that they considered you as much their daughter as they did me then you can forget it. My father adored his only sister, your mother, but he considered your father an irresponsible young idiot who, if he hadn't killed both your mother and himself with his reckless driving, would sooner or later have shaken off the burden of a wife and daughter his own family were too snobbish to recognize and returned hotfoot to his ancestral home. Daddy has always considered him responsible for your mother's death and over the years you must have given him many anguished moments, because, according to Mummy, you've inherited his looks to an astonishing degree. Not that they're anything much to shout about,' she added spitefully, glancing into an oval mirror that sparkled back a reassuring reflection, 'your only worthwhile inheritance is a coil of golden hair. How much richer our childhood would have been if only your golden inheritance could have lined our pockets!'

'I don't agree,' Lucille answered quietly. 'Thanks to Uncle Peter and Aunt Marion I had a wonderful childhood—and so did you.' Gently she urged, 'Surely you haven't forgotten the happy times we spent together, the picnics, the holidays, the exciting Christmases . . .?'

For a second she thought Shani was about to soften; her cousin's back was turned, but something in the stillness of her body, in the slight sideways cocking of her head, suggested that she might be remembering half-forgotten carols sung around a tree glistening with lights, or the sound of laughter which, in retrospect, had seemed to fill the modest semi every day of their young lives.

Then the slender shoulders shrugged and the moment was lost. 'Nonsense!' Shani swung on her heel, her eyes greedily encompassing the luxury surrounding her. 'It might suit you to ignore the fact that in those days we were practically penniless, but I'll never forget that when everyone else was holidaying abroad we had to be content with a week at a holiday camp—and a self-catering one at that! No, my dear simpleton, life only began for me when I left drama school. One lucky break was all I needed —that, and the determination to reach the top as quickly as possible and to stay there. Nothing can stop me now,' she glittered, her green eyes narrow with intent. 'Just one more rung of the ladder to scale until the absolute pinnacle is reached, and with Tareq Hawke as my co-star it's as good as done!' She laughed, a sudden harsh laugh that made Lucille jump. 'Don't pretend you aren't pleased that you hitched your wagon to a star,' she mocked, revelling in the knowledge of power. 'I can't say I've noticed any reluctance on your part to savour the pleasures that money can buy. Consider yourself lucky, Lucy Lamb, that sentiment forces me to overlook your many acts of incompetence because only the fact that I know my parents would be distressed has prevented me from getting rid of you long ago!'

She swept out, leaving Lucille to digest the threat behind her words. It was not the first warning she had been given that her services might soon become superfluous, but of late Shani's ever-present resentment had become more marked and so the threat must finally be heeded. Obviously her presence grated upon Shani, but why she had no idea. Always, she tried to be unobtrusive, and although she was never given credit or praise she knew she was both competent and efficient in her job. No, Shani's animosity had a personal significance which went deeper than her words implied. She had been quite right in asserting that any break between them would cause her parents anxiety, but for a different reason from the one stated. Knowing their own spoiled, wilful child, they had begged Lucille to accept the job as companion in the hope that some of the dignified reserve they so admired in their niece might rub off on their daughter. Lucille had felt unable to refuse the only return she had ever been asked for a lifetime of love and security so unwillingly she had agreed. But right from the beginning the relationship had been a strain. Shani's resentment, her avaricious desire for more and more money, and the dislike she no longer made any effort to hide was making life progressively harder

13

to bear.

But Lucille had another reason for wanting to accomplish just one more voyage before the break finally came. Whatever insults or slights Shani felt disposed to inflict would have to be borne in silence, meekly, and without sign of rebellion. Even if, at times, she might appear to speculative onlookers to have descended to the rank of a Victorian domestic, pride would have to be swallowed and embarrassment hidden if she were to deprive Shani of the concrete cause for dismissal she was so obviously seeking.

As expected, a full-scale row erupted when Art Callahan arrived. As he sipped the whisky Shani had dispensed from a crystal decanter, his glittering eyes belied the attitude of relaxation engendered by the sight of his sprawled limbs cosseted within the depths of an armchair.

'You could be having me on, I suppose, Shani, the pretence of having booked this floating mansion for the whole of the voyage is just the sort of idiotic legpull I've come to expect of you. So all right, you've had your fun—now tell me,' he smiled thinly, 'that this is just another example of your way-out humour!'

'Humour be damned!' she snapped, revolving from the drinks tray so that he received the full benefit of her glowering look. 'For too long I've put up with second-class travel, endured diabolical discomfort and endlessly boring journeys because of your insistence upon keeping within a budget. But no longer! Now that I'm a star I'll do the insisting, and if the studio don't like it they can cancel my contract!' Their eyes clashed, the dislike between them needless of words. Shani's smile was a thread of silken assurance when she challenged, 'There are other studios eager to employ me, Art—studios who don't quibble about paying up to keep their protegés happy ...'

He hooked a long leg across his knee and studied the sole of his shoe in silence. Lucille waited, tense as a high note, for his verdict. Too much progress had been made on the preliminary preparations for the forthcoming film to abandon it completely, more money would be wasted than saved if he should call Shani's bluff by insisting upon a less extravagant form of transport.

When he decided to employ sweet reason she expelled a relieved breath. 'I didn't quibble when you informed me of your intention to travel part of the journey by cruise ship,' he contradicted mildly, 'not even when it meant subjecting everyone to the inconvenience of disembarking at Mombasa to continue to Cairo by air. You must have known how long it would take, yet still you insisted upon doing things your way even though we could have accomplished the whole of the journey to Cairo by air in a matter of hours.'

'And for fewer coppers!' Shani scoffed. 'That would have suited you fine, wouldn't it? Well, it's no go. Either you agree to pay the full expenses of this trip or you can tear up my contract here and now!'

Silence fell after the ultimatum, a silence which was eventually broken by the sound of footsteps proceeding along the alleyway and stopping outside the door of the adjoining suite. There was a clinking sound as silver changed hands, murmured thanks from a grateful steward, then the firm closing of a door.

'Well, well,' Shani murmured, 'it sounds as if my famous co-star has finally arrived! What about it, Art, do I tell him the film's off, or will you?'

Art rose to his feet, his lean frame deprived of energy, his features grim with defeat. 'There's nothing to tell,' he conceded bitterly, 'but even if there were legend has it that the Hawk is no mean expert at finding out things for himself!'

CHAPTER TWO

EIGHT hours had passed by the time Lucille had accomplished the avalanche of tasks Shani had set her, so that when finally she was free to sink her aching limbs into the depth of an armchair the liner had progressed from Southampton to Cherbourg and was set on course for New York. She leant back her head and closed her eyes, grateful for the solitude of the small writing-room she had found tucked away in a quiet corner of the ship. Thankfully, she comforted herself that she had no need to dress for dinner, a chore peculiar to first-class passengers who appeared almost unanimous in their agreement that the grandeur of the Queen's Grill warranted the effort of donning evening dress even on the first night out.

'Found you at last, Elusive Lucy! Where the devil have you been all day?'

Smothering a groan of annoyance, she prised open reluctant eyelids and was confronted by Art's large grin. Everything about him was large. Limbs loose-jointed and awkward; mouth generous and kind, and a heart equally proportioned to accommodate the affection he dispensed with such discrimination that few, if any, of his cliché of celluloid stars were even aware it existed. Lucille was one of the favoured few. As his talents had been so speedily recognized, success had caught him unawares so that although mentally brilliant he had to strive perpetually to hide from his shrewd stars the sense of youthful inadequacy that plagued him. He often sought her out when he felt in need of support, to be soothed by her sympathy and understanding before once more donning the cloak of ruthlessness so necessary to his rôle of director of temperamental artistes.

'You haven't been avoiding me deliberately, have you?' he queried suspiciously as he sank into an adjacent chair.

'As if I would!' she retorted, scrambling erect lest her listlessness should be mistaken for disinterest. 'I'm always glad to see you, Art, you're the only *real* person in the whole of this travelling menagerie!'

He howled with amusement, then spluttered. 'You're full of surprises, my sweet! Don't ever allow the *menagerie* to suspect that the lamb in its midst has claws—I wouldn't fancy your chances against that green-eyed cat, Shani, nor even against the Hawk, for all his reputed chivalry towards the weaker sex!'

She shrugged, unable to cull up the slightest interest in any member of a profession she had come to regard as the ultimate in artifice. Granted, escapism was the object of their undoubted talent, but the adulation of their fans did nothing to discourage a conceit which all too often resulted in turning flesh-and-blood people into shadows dancing on a screen, imitative puppets—with minds to match.

Sensing her trend of thought, Art frowned. 'Don't fall into the error of judging all movie stars by your experiences of Shani and her followers. Tareq Hawke, for instance——'

'—Is just another fantasy hero!' She yawned, suddenly bored with the subject. 'As the son of a wealthy family and a product of one of the best schools in Cairo, he could have become something of a scholastic celebrity or even a sportsman of distinction, but he opted instead to be a gambler, a womanizer, a big spender. He's the kind of star Hollywood gossips love to mate, an Aswan Dam of sex who's had more beautiful women thrown his way than a computer could count! Without ever having met him,' she heaved out of her chair, 'I'm willing to bet that if there were Oscars for sheer conceit he'd win one annually!'

'I say, that's a bit strong . . .!' Art protested.

'I'm going in to dinner,' she interrupted firmly, 'have you eaten?'

Recognizing adamant refusal to continue with the argument, he capitulated. 'No, I haven't, we'll dine together.' But when they reached the end of the alleyway and he ushered her in the direction of the Queen's Grill he was amazed when she shook him off and pointed in the opposite direction.

'My dining-room is this way, perhaps we can meet for a drink later?'

Like a steel trap his jaws snapped together. 'Are you telling me Shani has had the nerve to book you into tourist class accommodation?'

'I prefer it,' she assured him, her small face a serious oval. 'Honestly, Art, I hate having to dress for dinner and the people in Tourist are so much more interesting—please don't make a fuss.'

'No fuss,' he promised through clenched teeth, exerting pressure on her arm as she tried to pull away, 'just a quick word to whoever's in charge of the Bureau so they can arrange to have your baggage moved into a first-class cabin while we're having dinner.'

He would not listen to further protest—to pleading even—and when Lucille finally realized that beneath a calm exterior he was seething she ceased resisting and requested in a small voice, 'Then at least give me time to change. I can't dine in the Queen's Grill wearing this old thing.' Reluctantly, he released her arm, recognizing the feasibility of her argument, and she sped along the alleyway to her cabin, leaving him to go in search of the chief purser.

Impatient with Art, and filled with self-annoyance at not having made her disappearance more complete, she rifled her wardrobe for the most unbecoming dress she could find, a colourless swathe of nylon chiffon that had acted as a wonderful foil for Shani's green eyes and fiery hair but which did nothing at all for the creamy delicacy of her cameo features. Hastily she threw it over her head, at the same time groping towards the dressing-table where comb and brush awaited the inevitable contact with ruffled hair. She emerged breathless from the diaphanous cloud that settled around her shoulders, contrasting barely at all—cream and ivory merging like two shades of pearl. Constant practice made easy the disciplining of the golden coil that she brushed smooth, then twisted into a prim bun positioned low upon the nape of her slender neck. No jewellery, no make-up, except for the merest touch of pink against her lips, and she was ready.

A fist rapping against the door sent her scurrying to the wardrobe. 'All right, I'm coming!' she replied to the commanding knock, slipping her feet into slender sandals and grabbing a matching evening bag before hurrying towards the door. Art was frowning, eyebrows beetling with displeasure as he prowled the alleyway, but his features lightened and good humour was re-established when he noted her flushed cheeks and breathless appearance.

'It's all fixed,' he grinned. 'During dinner your things will be moved into a cabin near to mine on One Deck and naturally we'll sit together for meals.'

'Thank you, Art,' she surrendered gracefully, helpless in the face of his determination. 'I only hope Shani won't take exception and cause a fuss.'

'She can make as much fuss as she likes,' he retorted grimly. 'Just leave Madame to me!'

But when they reached the Queen's Grill it became immediately obvious that Shani's attention lay in a different direction. She was oblivious to all but her companion, the man sharing her table. Conversation was washing around them, but the pair were wrapped in isolation, immune to the waves of chatter that would have intruded upon their privacy, completely absorbed in the exploration of each other's personality. Shani was doing most of the talking, holding his attention with flirtatious upward glances from eyes sparkling green with excitement, her beautiful mouth a butterfly of crimson pouting prettily against a contrasting petal-white complexion.

Her companion's dark head was inclined downward to catch her every word. Thick black lashes screened eyes that seemed to hold in their depths a thousand nocturnal secrets, secrets cherished for his

21

own entertainment so that should he ever become slightly bored only a retrospective glance into his past would be needed to revive the quirk of amusement that seemed to live permanently on his lips. He had the tan of an Arab and the features of an autocrat, self-willed mouth, flaring nostrils, and a haughty turn of head probably inherited from his French father. It had been said, Lucille recalled, that his mother was a Moroccan princess, but then so much fantasy had been woven around the handsome Tareq Hawke ... His voice, however, held the timbre and cadences of a race familiar with legions of space through which the softly spoken word echoed clearly from desert floor to star-shot ceiling. He was supremely self-assured, an assurance which Lucille had no doubt was born of a profound knowledge of his favourite subject—women!

'Shani seems well and truly hooked,' Art offered casually as he ushered Lucille to a nearby table, 'but she's wasting her time, I'm afraid. Tareq is not averse to a casual flirtation, but he's far too wary to allow himself to become deeply involved.' Lucille was glad when they were seated at their table and the subject of Tareq Hawke was displaced by the more serious topic of what to choose from the menu. Waiters were hastening backwards and forwards between the tables carrying offerings to tempt the appetites of even the most fastidious of diners. Globules of citrus fruit bloomed in silver dishes under light cast from enormous circular shades of cut glass closely attached to a royal blue ceiling. Ruffled drapes of a deeper shade of blue added depth of comfort to a room devoted to the serving of excellent food in superb surroundings, a place to linger over wine poured into slim-stemmed glasses by hovering stewards whose main purpose in life seemed to be the complete satisfaction of their particular diners.

'Well, what shall we order?' Art handed her a menu and leant back, relaxed and happy, to study his own in comfort.

'Grapefruit to begin with, I think,' she decided, then with a chuckle of delight, 'and Guinness and oyster soup sounds interesting!'

'Followed by duckling in orange sauce, then almond meringue!' Art finished triumphantly. When she nodded enthusiastic support he gave the order, then leant forward to study her thoughtfully. 'You're great fun to be with—do you know that? No tantrums, no scenes, no looking into a mirror on every conceivable occasion. To me, you're like a draught of delicious cool water after a surfeit of champagne.'

'Thank you for nothing!' she quipped, pretending offence at the back-handed compliment.

Immediately he was contrite. 'Lucy, don't get me wrong, I didn't mean ...' then belatedly he noticed the twinkle adding sparkle to her grey eyes and the undisciplined dimple coming and going at the corner of her mouth. 'You knew what I meant, you teasing little devil. I've half a mind to spank you for that!' As she gurgled with laughter he reached across the table and caught hold of her hand, retaliating by squeezing deliberately hard. Determined not to betray discomfort, she was laughingly protesting her innocence when Shani's furious voice startled them apart.

'If you two must play idiotic games would you

kindly do so in private? And what, may-I ask, are you doing in here, Lucille? Shouldn't you be dining in one of the other restaurants?'

Sheer humiliation drove Lucille to her feet much to Art's annoyance. 'I'm sorry, Art had my cabin changed ...' The apology dried in her throat, parched by the amusement of the man at Shani's side, intent and wholly interested, his half narrowed eyes taking inventory as he prepared to enjoy any diversion, however momentary. When her glance flickered in his direction his lips quirked and she looked away, intensely resenting his casual, almost bored involvement in her affairs.

Shani's furious eyes collided with Art's and for a few seconds sparks flashed between them, then when Art's jutting jaw registered intention to pull rank, she resisted the temptation to make a scene and turned instead to direct her spite against Lucille.

'I need you in my suite right away,' she commanded. 'Some of the dresses I intend wearing tomorrow are only half pressed. Every crease must be removed before you can consider yourself off duty.'

The coil of golden hair seemed almost too heavy for the slender neck bowed under the indignity of being made to appear servile. Terribly conscious of Tareq Hawke's raised eyebrows and of Art's silent urging to rebel, Lucille drew in a shaky breath and exposed Shani to a cool grey gaze. 'Very well, if you'll excuse me, I'll see to them now.'

'But I've ordered dinner!' Art exploded. 'Really, Shani, you ask too much. Lucille's already put in a ten-hour working day!'

Coolly Shani smiled, linking her arm through her companion's, whose features were unreadable. 'She

24

isn't a slave chained by the ankle. If the conditions of employment don't suit her she's perfectly free to go ...!' The challenge was flung at Lucille's feet and she could sense them waiting for some show of spirit, some effort to assert her rights, but too much was at stake. Flinching from Art's incredulous look, she ignored Shani's ultimatum and agreed:

'If there is work to be done, then of course I must do it. I'm sorry about dinner, Art, please don't wait for me.' Without waiting to hear further argument, she grabbed her evening bag and ran—supposedly towards the suite, but actually away from the sight of Shani's triumph, Art's furious amazement and Tareq Hawke's visible contempt.

Once inside the suite she took herself furiously to task as she swept up the pile of dresses Shani had left crumpled on the floor and began preparations to iron out the deliberately inflicted creases. 'Why bother what any of them think?' she berated through clenched teeth. 'Once this trip is over you'll be free, my girl, so you must look upon these next few weeks as a baptism of fire which must be endured for the sake of being reborn!'

She had almost finished and was just clearing away when Shani's high-pitched laughter penetrated from outside the suite. A key scraped in the lock and Lucille was cornered before she could attempt an escape.

'But I insist, darling!' Lucille heard her say, 'Nothing would give me more pleasure than to have you share the services of my employee. She's yours whenever you want her!'

Blood pounded in Lucille's ears as she swung on her heel to meet the piercing eyes of Tareq Hawke.

He was lounging in the doorway, thoughtfully contemplating the merchandise he had just been offered, half frowning, half impatient—she felt like a slave girl in a market place suffering the inspection of a prospective buyer! Colour fired her body as his assessment continued, his glances leaving scorching trails where they lingered over perfect curves.

'We must come to some arrangement about payment.' Through roaring in her ears Lucille heard the outrageous remark tossed casually across his shoulder.

'Don't be silly, darling!' Shani's laughter floated through from the adjoining room. 'Feel free to make use of anything she has to offer!'

Lucille's scandalized eyes grew wider as she fought to suppress words that would have put paid to her dearest ambition if indignation had allowed her to find her voice. But, seemingly unconscious of the tirade struggling to find expression, he straightened and lazily drawled, 'Only shorthand and typing ability is required,' he cocked an eyebrow, 'provided, of course, that you, Miss Lamb, have no objection to helping me out until my own secretary is well enough to join us in Cairo?'

Her heartfelt gasp of relief brought dawning amusement to his aquiline features. Obviously, her naïveté had entertained him, and she was furious with herself for allowing him to guess that she had thought his motives suspect. He addressed her directly, but with hidden innuendo. 'May I take it that you are willing, Miss Lamb?' he ridiculed, watching keenly the waves of colour firing her cheeks. It was at that precise moment that she began to hate him—a curious reaction from one who hitherto had felt unable to award to any member of his profession so much as a passing interest ...

'If I can be of service, monsieur,' she answered stiffly, 'and since Shani has no objection, then of course I shall be pleased to help out whenever I can.'

For long seconds his glance jabbed like a pin directly on the spot where her lip had begun a scornful curl, but when her mouth was hastily controlled he nodded approval, then dismissed her with the curt instruction, 'Good, present yourself in my suite at ten tomorrow morning.'

She was still seething when Art found her an hour later hanging over the ship's rail yearning, for some unspecified reason, for the nerve to slip quietly over the side and be swallowed into dark, anonymous depths. Without speaking, he leant next to her and joined her silent contemplation of rushing water, then when she showed no sign of resenting his intrusion he forced out the accusation: 'Why do you let her get away with it, Lucille?'

She did not pretend to misunderstand. 'I need the job, Art, it's as simple as that.' She was surprised when he did not object. She had expected recrimination, a slating even, for her spineless lack of initiative, but when the silence remained unbroken she sighed and continued her vigil.

Then out of the darkness his voice reached strained but deeply sincere. 'Lucy, will you marry me? Wait, let me finish——' he blocked her startled protest. 'I know we're not in love, but we get along famously and we've lots of interests in common. This, to me, augurs well for matrimonial harmony. As you know, I'm against marriage between members of the theatrical profession—seen too many founder on the rocks of selfishness and fading physical attraction—but you know all about this kind of life, you're unflappable, good-natured, calm in an emergency. Living out of a suitcase doesn't seem to bother you, so there'd be none of the scenes I might expect from any other woman unused to this travelling circus. But besides all that,' he paused to breathe in deeply, 'it would save you the worry of finding another job . . .'

'Oh, Art!' was the only reply she could make to his generous offer. He was right, they were not in love, nor were they ever likely to be, but right at that moment she adored him for his thoughtful gesture, a gesture so kind it could be repaid only with complete honesty. Reaching out to touch his hand, she asked softly, 'Can you keep a secret?' He gave a puzzled nod. 'Very well, then I'll try to explain.'

A trill of excitement ran in her voice as she told him. 'About a year ago I began submitting articles to a magazine, and the success I achieved encouraged me to venture into more ambitious fields. Using the wealth of materials stored from my travels with Shani, I began writing a book—not the usual travelogue, but more of an insight into the manners and customs of people of different lands. Well, to cut a long story short, I sent along the first few chapters to a publisher and to my delight he was interested, so interested that he's given me a firm promise of publication once the book is completed. There's just one snag,' she informed an astonished Art, 'the last chapter deals with the Arab race and their customs, so perhaps now you can understand why on no account must I be prevented from doing the necessary research in Egypt.'

Above the sound of churning water she heard his gasp of amazement, then his voice came, warmly congratulatory, words stumbling over themselves with surprise. 'You little dark horse! I always suspected there was more to you than meets the eye, but this . . .! Congratulations, sweetheart, and thank you for taking me into your confidence. You've explained a lot . . .'

'Please don't repeat what I've told you to anyone, Art,' she urged hastily. 'I've barely had time to get used to the idea myself and I couldn't bear it if Shani should find out and begin to scoff.' She began to stammer. 'If . . . if my book is a success I mean to give up my job and concentrate entirely upon writing, but if it isn't . . .' She left unsaid the unbearable alternative. For the first time in her life independence beckoned on the horizon—but what if it should turn out to be a tantalizing mirage?

'You *will* succeed, I know it!' Art assured her. 'Don't worry about having the opportunity to do the necessary research. As we're already on our way, what can possibly prevent you from reaching Egypt now?'

CHAPTER THREE

TAREQ HAWKE'S suite was a luxurious twin of the one occupied by Shani, more masculine in appeal but equally sumptuous in appointment. Lucille hesitated on the threshold, loath to set foot on the sea of rich red carpet flowing under armchairs generously tailored to accommodate a long-legged frame, occasional tables set square to resist the impact of broad strides and a desk delicately designed in walnut and brass which for all its beauty was primarily functional. She coughed; the door was open, but there was no sign of the dictator who had ordered her presence in his suite the night before. She was about to turn tail and run when his voice penetrated downward from the direction of the upper floor bedroom. 'Make yourself comfortable, Mademoiselle Lamb. I'll be with you in a minute!'

Clutching her notebook as if it were a talisman against the evil eye, she ventured into his lair and perched nervously on the edge of a tapestried chair. Her attention was caught by a huge oil painting which she thought might be a likeness of Lady Hamilton; tentatively she stood up and tiptoed across to read the small plaque set into the gilt frame.

'Ah, *la belle* Emma! She was your complete antithesis, mademoiselle!' She spun round to find him studying the portrait across her shoulder. 'For me there are only two kinds of women,' he continued lazily, 'goddesses and doormats!'

Scarlet-cheeked, Lucille digested the pleasantly voiced insult, but decided not to allow him the satisfaction of arousing her resentment. Her voice echoed with the implied subordination when she questioned nervously, 'Do you wish to begin dictating, monsieur? If so, I have my notebook ready.'

'So I see.' He moved easily towards the telephone. 'First of all we will have some coffee.' She fidgeted while he put through a call to the steward, wishing only to get his dictation down on paper so that she might escape his disturbing presence. Her own feelings surprised her; immune as she was to the studied actions of his professional colleagues, it was confusing to be confronted by one who did not conform, a puzzling enigma who played lazily on the edge of life but who nevertheless was capable of surgically accurate observations. Under the pretext of sharpening her pencil she watched under lowered lids as he prowled the room. His dress was impeccable, hand-tailored slacks and slim-fitting shirt moulded a form sleek as a desert cat, but not even Savile Row expertise could camouflage the thrust of powerful shoulders and the physical perfection of limbs fluid in motion. He stalked rather than walked, a gorgeous animal, sharp-eyed and sleek, with nothing about him pertaining to either the cosy or the comfortable.

When the coffee arrived she poured out, then handed him his cup with all the delicacy of an ingénue confronted for the first time by the savagely unpredictable.

'Tell me,' he sounded exasperated as he accepted the proffered cup from hands that trembled, 'are you always so timid, or are you *really* expecting me to bite?'

As no answer presented itself she remained silent, incapable of explaining even to herself the tingle of fear and excitement that had raced through her veins when their fingers touched. A mild oath ripped above her apprehensive head, the curse effective enough to send startled eyes riveting upon his face. Without understanding why, Lucille sensed that he was very angry, but she was totally unprepared for the verbal lashing he rained upon her defenceless head.

'One of my greatest problems,' he projected through clenched teeth, 'is trying to live up to my reputation! Every woman I meet expects me to be the greatest lover in the world, like you, they expect to be swept up and torn apart by an Egyptian savage ...!' Her indignant denial was annihilated by his brutal insistence upon being heard out. 'Once, I would not have found this challenge daunting, but to have to live through the experience of a thousand and one such nights is beyond the capacity of any male. I get a little weary of finding notes slipped under my door saying things like: "Saw you in the bar. Please say you'll have dinner with me." Indeed, in time it becomes decidedly boring, because once I've worked my way around the dozen or so women on offer there's really little else to do but begin again at the beginning!'

Suddenly he stopped pacing and a glance into her strained face seemed to douse the fire within him. Leaning from his great height, he pinched her chin between a thumb and forefinger, forcing a look from embarrassed grey eyes. 'I'm sorry if I've shocked you, mademoiselle, but it was necessary if we are to work together. Harmony is an essential ingredient of everyday happiness, but such harmony could never have existed had you remained nervous in my presence or suspicious of my intentions.'

He straightened to saunter across to the desk where a pile of letters awaited his attention, giving her time to compose her feelings, but then he shattered them still further with the caustic observation. 'Now that you have been assured that I have no designs on your virtue, perhaps we can commence work?'

It required great strength of will to pick up her notebook and pencil and act as if nothing of consequence had passed between them. Beneath her calm exterior she was fighting to regain the breath knocked out of her by a declaration so insensitive she felt soiled by it. She was used to blunt speaking. Shani's friends were all sophisticated and informed, their conversation a brittle battle of wits revolving mainly around feminine emancipation and the alleged equality of the sexes—but his allegations were so unbelievably conceited she could not help but feel a sudden stirring of partisanship for her much maligned sex.

But as the morning progressed it became increasingly obvious that he had not exaggerated the extent of his problem. Most of his mail was made up of letters from adoring women which he insisted upon reading aloud before dictating a stereotyped reply. Lucille's cheeks were afire when finally he handed over the letters so that she might refer to individual addresses, but his look was sardonic, a look that challenged her to prove for herself that the extremely intimate passages he had read out were fact before condemning him as an egotistical male with an exaggerated opinion of his own attraction.

Working between two masters, Lucille was kept so busy during the next couple of weeks that she barely had time to eat, much less enjoy the leisurely mealtimes Art had planned. No sooner had she worked her way through one stack of mail than the ship would reach port to take on yet another pile, seemingly larger than the last, and the whole wearying process would begin again. Each morning after breakfast she went to Tareq Hawke's suite to transcribe two hours of dictation, then after lunch it was Shani's turn to claim her for a procession of jobs which she delighted in prolonging so far into the evening that Lucille usually had a scramble to get dressed for dinner. What was left of the day was utilised typing out the letters dictated earlier, so that by the time the ship had almost reached Rio de Janeiro they had been at sea for eighteen days, calling at New York, Curaçao and Salvador Bahia on the way, yet all she had seen was the inside of the restaurant, her own cabin and the suites of Shani and Tareq Hawke.

Art was the first to comment on her wan features and air of fatigue. She was sorting through tights, examining them for snags while Shani was taking a shower and probably thinking up more ways to keep her companion occupied while she herself enjoyed the superb facilities of the luxury ship. He was lounging in a chair waiting to discuss some aspect of the new film with Shani, and his eyes narrowed when Lucille, totally absorbed, paused to press taut fingers against her throbbing temples. The action triggered off the fury he had been feeling

34

on her behalf and precipitated an explosion.

'Lucy, you've done enough for one day. Put down those damned tights and relax while I pour you a drink!'

'In a minute,' she replied absently, 'but it will have to be a small one. I haven't time to . . .'

'Make time!' he barked, suddenly unreasonably irritated by her devotion to duty. 'For heaven's sake, you're not a domestic, and these aren't the Dark Ages! The most menial employee on this ship has had more time off since we sailed, so I insist you stop pandering to Shani's selfishness before you collapse from sheer exhaustion!'

The extent of her tiredness was demonstrated when her eyes filled with tears so unexpected she had no time to hide them. Perversely, she put the blame for her lapse upon his solicitude and snapped back, 'I don't care if I'm reduced to a shadow. Shani mustn't become upset, and I don't have to remind you why!'

Her worried earnestness made him feel shame and his manner softened. 'Look, sweetheart, there's no sense in working yourself to death. Give Shani notice, let me pay your expenses for this trip so that you can gather material for your book and enjoy yourself in the process. Call it a loan, if you insist,' he hastened to add when her forehead puckered. 'You can pay me back when the royalties start rolling in.'

For a second her face brightened, then slowly she shook her head. 'No, thank you, Art,' she declined firmly, 'I couldn't possibly accept your offer when I'm so short of security. You're very kind, but you're also very optimistic, because if the book should flop the money could never be returned, and I couldn't bear to live with that on my conscience. At least, this way, I'm working my passage.'

He sighed, knowing better than to argue. 'Then take tonight off,' he pleaded. 'We could tour the bars, have a flutter in the casino, visit a cabaret or a night club—I'll even take you to see a film, if you insist,' he finished desperately.

She had to laugh. The idea of Art sitting through someone else's film when he had the planning of his own on his mind was the ultimate in self-sacrifice and demanded a favourable response. 'Very well,' she accepted, feeling suddenly light-headed, 'I'll say yes to everything except the film!'

She dressed carefully for the evening ahead. Every dress she owned was a cast-off of Shani's, their acceptance necessary because of the scarcity of a monthly salary cheque and the frugality of those few that did finally manage to come her way. The small amounts she received from publishers of magazines that had accepted her articles were used mainly for items such as underwear and the remainder was hoarded and used as pocket money on the few occasions she was allowed enough time off to join excursions or trips ashore. The dress she chose was a favourite, a starkly simple sheath, blue as a patch of desert sky—an impulse buy of Shani's that had been hastily discarded without ever being worn. Lucille pirouetted in front of a mirror, pleased with the way the cleverly cut material clung to her body, adding mature elegance to her young curves. A pair of tiny silver earrings guiltily purchased in an Italian market place matched the dress perfectly and nestled against pale velvet earlobes to draw the eye wonderingly along a delicate profile made to look even finer by the constrasting density of a rope of pale golden hair.

Art's admiration had no need of words when he arrived carrying a transparent box containing a corsage made up of one perfect white rose. 'For you, princess,' he offered, smiling down at her flushed, expectant face.

'Oh, Art, you're spoiling me!'

'Time someone did,' he replied gruffly, assisting with the release of the captive flower. 'As I see it, you were intended merely to sit upon a cushion sewing fine seams, not wearing yourself to a frazzle in the service of others less sensitive than yourself.' But Lucille was busy pinning on the corsage, excited at the prospect of the pleasures ahead, so the observation which she would have gently ridiculed was disregarded.

What began initially as a prowl around the night spots soon developed into a conducted tour of the ship, her enthusiasm propelling them from one deck to another as she pandered to her appetite for the unusual and the unknown. They peeped into each of the nine bars—Art being allowed time for a drink in only two of them—then progressed by way of many lifts to discover four swimming pools, two magnificently stocked libraries, a theatre, an arcade of shops stocking such fabulous merchandise that he thought she would become glued permanently before the display, then finally to a casino on the upper deck where excitement hovered like an electric force above green baize tables as fortunes ebbed and flowed between croupiers and punters. It was there that Art dug in his heels and refused to budge.

Depositing her firmly in a seat at the bar, he glinted, 'Not one more step do I move until I've had a drink, perhaps two—who knows how many it will take to ease the agony of a pair of feet assaulted by contact with miles of hard deck when previously they've known only the gentle contact of deep carpet!'

'Sorry,' she gurgled. 'I've no wish to spoil your evening, I'm having a *wonderful* time!' He relented, no proof against the sparkling enjoyment that had bestowed extreme beauty upon his companion. But as they sipped their drinks her expression of animation faded and quickly she turned her back on the crowded tables and began toying with the glass holding her frosted drink.

'Something wrong?' Art questioned anxiously, trying unsuccessfully to probe behind downcast lashes. Lucille shrugged, searching for words to appease his anxiety and finding none. She was angry with herself for displaying obvious emotion; how could she even begin to explain to someone as matter-of-fact as Art that the swift quenching of her enjoyment had been brought about merely by the sight of a familiar pair of shoulders, the set of an arrogant head, and the sharp incisiveness of a look completely attendant at the moment upon the caprice of a nearby roulette wheel? Explanation was impossible, so she resorted to the age-old excuse of Eve.

'I have a headache ... would you mind ...?'

Immediately he was full of concern. 'Of course not, princess. I'll see you to your cabin and chase someone along with tablets to ease the pain.' She felt treacherous taking advantage of his kindness, but then suffered sudden retribution when tiny spasms of pain began throbbing at her temples and her limbs felt weighted with a tiredness so pressing she was no longer called upon to pretend.

But if she had thought herself released once Art had left her to the ministrations of a kindly stewardess she soon learned otherwise. No sooner had she slipped into a dressing-gown than a tap at the door heralded a messenger with a request that she present herself in Shani's suite right away. Wondering why she was wanted at such a late hour, she hurried along the alleyway to the suite, anxiously examining her day's actions for some clue to prepare her for whatever lay ahead.

Shani was pacing the floor with the attitude of an enraged tiger, conscious even in wrath of the flattering effect fury lent to her green eyes and passionately beautiful face.

'How dare he!' she flung at Lucille the moment she appeared. 'How dare that fugitive from the desert treat me as if I were a concubine awaiting the favour of his attention? Three hours I've waited!' she informed an astonished Lucille, 'and what do you suppose has superseded his dinner date with me?' Lucille shook her head. 'None other than roulette, dice and blackjack, that's what! I've just been informed that all this time I've been waiting, thinking up excuses for his non-appearance, he's been raking in a small fortune at the tables!'

Lucille cleared an obstruction from her throat. 'You certainly have cause to complain. Monsieur Hawke's manners are usually impeccable, but if he made a firm arrangement with you and then failed to turn up . . .'

'Arrangement? Don't be stupid, arrangements are not necessary between Tareq and myself. It's been understood from the moment we boarded ship that we would spend every available moment together!'

'I see . . .' Lucille felt some reply was expected of her.

'I doubt it!' Shani's lips pursed contemptuously. 'Your life has been lived on too humdrum a plane to allow you to even marginally comprehend the violent emotions spawned by the mating of two such explosive characters as Tareq and myself.' She preened, smoothing complacent hands across her hips, anger completely routed. 'I intend to marry him,' she stated calmly. 'He'll make a magnificent mate, aggravating, but never dull.' She gave an exultant laugh. 'We'll fight, of course, then we'll make up—but only when it suits *me*. Whether or not he cares to admit it, Tareq the Hawk, for the first time in his life, has encountered an attraction powerful enough to become troublesome.' She swung round to challenge Lucille with the unanswerable. 'Why else would he be avoiding me, were it not that he's uncertain of his ability to resist capture?'

CHAPTER FOUR

WHEN Lucille awoke the next morning the coast of Rio de Janeiro was etched upon the skyline. She stood glued to the porthole as the ship approached the breathtakingly beautiful city lying at the foot of high green mountains rising abruptly from sea and bay. White beaches stretched in graceful curves all along the coast, and standing back from the beaches she could just make out the outlines of modern appartments, hotels, and various public buildings. High above, the Sugar Loaf Mountain stood guard at the entrance to the bay and towering over the whole city was the Hunchback Mountain from which a colossal statue of Christ with arms open wide looked benignly down. She lingered so long she was almost late for breakfast and Shani and Art were just preparing to leave the dining-room when she made her breathless entrance.

'Where have you been?' Shani snapped irritably. 'Today of all days you might have made an effort to rise earlier!'

'I'm sorry,' Lucille mumbled apologetically, 'I had no idea you'd be needing me at such an early hour.'

'Of course you were needed!' Shani glowered, pulling on a pair of long white gloves before smoothing down the skirt of her most elegant outfit. 'Today, Art and I have to appear at a full round of press conferences, cocktail parties and lunches arranged months ago by the publicity boys—you surely can't have forgotten?'

Lucille could barely disguise rising excitement as, carefully casual, she asked, 'Does that mean I won't be wanted for the rest of today?'

Shani stared suspiciously, then, acting upon the assumption that Lucille was disappointed at not having been asked to join them, she took great pleasure in replying.

'I'm afraid not. Your presence would be entirely superfluous, so I suggest that as you're remaining aboard you present yourself before Tareq with my instructions that you're to carry out whatever duties he might demand of you.'

Disappointment welled up inside Lucille. For one glorious moment she had thought herself free to escape to the wonderful city beckoning so tantalizingly from across the water. She swallowed hard and did her best to smile when Art paused long enough to bid her farewell.

'Chin up, princess, meet me tonight in the Grill Room bar about eleven and we'll have a drink together.'

After a solitary breakfast Lucille made her way in the direction of Tareq Hawke's suite, silently berating the fact that being a star of such consequence he no longer had to seek publicity but rather had to devise ways of avoiding it. His hearing was as acute as his perception, she thought ruefully, as in answer to her softly reluctant knock he demanded: *'Entrez!'* Nervously she stepped inside, then halted, feet primly together, just across the threshold.

'Shani said ...' she began, then had to stop to clear her throat. 'I've come to do whatever you

Rio was *en fête*, celebrating one of the many local saints' festivals that were enjoyed enthusiastically throughout Brazil. Lucille forgot her shyness and listened avidly as Tareq explained the folk drama being enacted before a crowd cramming a square they had come upon quite by accident as they made their way from the harbour en route for the city centre. Most of the spectators were dressed in farmers' costumes, the women in flounced gingham dresses, their black hair decorated with flowers and ribbons, and the men in casual trousers and white shirts filled in at the neckline with brightly coloured neckerchiefs, their eyes shaded from the sun by broad-brimmed hats with straps that dangled beneath their chins.

'We are fortunate,' Tareq informed her, answering with a smile the questions teeming behind her wide-open eyes. 'Today is one of the Festivals of the Saints of June—either Anthony, John, Peter or Paul. In cities and towns this is a time for children to set off fireworks and for adults to hold dances and build bonfires around which they roast sweet potatoes and sing traditional songs. This small tableau is called *Boi-Bumba* and it is telling the ancient story of how a cowboy's ox was killed by Indians.'

A roar of laughter from the crowd coincided with a sudden swaying as people jostled forward seeking a better view of whatever it was that had caused their amusement. Annoyingly, Lucille found her view blocked by a burly pair of shoulders which even on tip-toe she could not negotiate. Immediately she was gripped by the waist and swung upwards on to Tareq's shoulder where, perched high above the sea of heads, she was presented with a perfect sight of the proceedings. Her lips parted to remonstrate against the indignity of her position, but then her attention was captured by the sight of a bull fashioned out of papier-mâché and cloth stretched over a bamboo frame inside which two men were in obvious difficulty.

The man who was animating the hindquarters had become very much out of step with his partner at the front, and their consequent efforts to right themselves had resulted in the bull-shaped frame developing contortions completely alien to either man or beast. The crowd's almost hysterical laughter was so infectious Lucille forgot her embarrassment and joined in, her enjoyment so complete she would have been in danger of falling from her perch had the hands that gripped her waist not held her secure. Tears of mirth were streaming down her cheeks by the time the tableau was finished and Tareq lowered her to the ground. Forgetting her animosity, she exchanged with him a smile of pure pleasure as she stood still as an obedient child and allowed him to mop her wet cheeks with a cool linen handkerchief.

'No need to ask if you enjoyed that, *chérie*! Even I who have seen it many times before am almost tempted to believe that the mishap was involuntary and not the well-rehearsed episode I know it to be.'

Some of her enjoyment died. 'I'm sad, *monsieur*, that cynicism has blunted your capacity for enjoyment.'

His smile was as tight as the grip on her arm as he began propelling her away from the square, his stride broadening so that she had to trot to keep up with his deliberately punishing pace.

For the rest of the day they assumed an attitude of armed neutrality, allowing no argument to spoil the pleasure easily available in a city determined to be gay, nor yet lowering their guard far enough to experience again the perfect accord they had achieved earlier. His speculative glances worried her, once or twice as they toured the city she felt his hard look, but she was too timid of reprisal to meet his eyes. It was not until later, while they prepared to dine in a discreetly luxurious restaurant heavily carpeted to deaden sound, and lighted only by individual lamps that cast around the occupants of each table a subdued circle of privacy, that his glances became less speculative and more indicative of inner satisfaction. Something in the air around her seemed to crackle a warning to beware as the leisurely dinner progressed and the half smiles her polite conversation were culling from his lips progressed into an expansive grin. He had made up his mind about something, she decided uneasily, but only time would tell whether her intuitive senses were correctly foretelling disaster.

His opening gambit was harmless enough, a preamble concerning his early days as a star. Lucille listened with faint interest as he admitted drifting idly into Cairo's flourishing Arab film world to discover that his gift of registering sadness had made him a star almost overnight.

'A film's success is reckoned by the volume of tears shed by the women in the audience,' he mocked, 'and that, I have found, holds good with women of the West as well as those of the East. Being an Egyptian actor in the western screen world has distinct advantages,' he mused. 'It makes one appear interesting—even exotic—and certainly versatile. So far, I've been cast in many different rôles and success has enabled me to indulge in my major vice—cards. But my father would never have approved. "Indulge all you like in drink and women", he once said, "but never play cards". However, drink makes one forgetful and women nag for remembrance, so rather than be totally ruined by either I chose to gamble!'

Her pulses responded to the reckless inflection in his voice, the tingling in her spine spelling out the message that far from indulging in the mere meanderings of an egotistical male his conversation was leading up to something.

'But now I've had enough!' he glittered accusingly. 'Enough of being labelled the screen's number one heart-throb! Enough of the so-called sweet life, of the everlasting merry-go-round of beautiful women, meetings, invitations, cruises, travel and filming! For six years I've travelled. Love affairs which might have led to something lasting have broken up because of my unstable way of life. Now I want peace, I want to work less, to settle down and marry someone gentle and serene, someone who'll act as a buffer against the female predators who stalk my footsteps, a homely housewife who'll give the cook the day off occasionally and prepare my supper and pander to my needs.'

He stopped to light a cheroot, obviously waiting for her reaction. Vacantly, she smiled, uncertain of what he expected, but his answering frown said it was not enough, so she strove desperately to revive some of the rather obvious clichés she had stored up in her mind for use on the many occasions when she had been called upon to act as blotting paper for the vapourings of other self-absorbed idols whose successes in the film world had made them dissatisfied with the realities of life.

'Well,' he barked, 'are you interested?'

'Yes, of course,' she stammered, unnerved by the steel-tipped glance that seemed to confound her theory of insecurity. 'Please do go on about your fascinating life.'

His stare was as disconcerting as the oath that escaped through clamped teeth. '*Sacré coeur*! I propose to you, and your only response is to attempt polite conversation!' With great effort of will he controlled his exasperation long enough to spell out. 'You, *mademoiselle*, go in constant fear of dismissal, undertaking the most menial of jobs because you are too timid to protest or to seek other employment, while I am in need of a female with the qualities I have just underlined. You fit my requirements admirably, so what do you say? Naturally, I shall not want you as a wife in the physical sense; all I want is a sort of—gentle protector—one whose presence cannot help but be noticed by any woman who might wish to trespass. Nevertheless, I would expect you to slide effortlessly into the background of my life without impinging upon my freedom to come and go as I choose. Materially, the rewards would be great,' he added as an afterthought. 'Besides having a house in Paris, I also have a villa in Portugal, a flat in London and a yacht anchored somewhere in the Mediterranean, so you see there is no longer any danger of my being seduced by fame and fortune!'

Vaguely, even in the midst of turmoil, Lucille found time to wonder from which parent he had inherited the startling blue eyes that were raking her stunned face. From his father, she decided: there was much of the dominating Gallic in the compelling glance that had her impaled as unmercifully as a butterfly on a pin and none of the compassion usually so eloquently expressed in the liquid brown eyes of his mother's race. She fought the attraction he subconsciously projected towards every member of her sex, despairing inwardly of controlling hands thrust under the table to hide their shaking and a heart that rose and fell erratically, dependent upon the whim of a lazily crooked eyebrow or the downward thrust of an impatient mouth.

She wondered if he suspected the panic hidden beneath her cool reply. 'You might at least have paid me the courtesy of being specific, Monsieur Hawke; it is not women *en masse* but one particular woman from whom you wish to run. But you're wasting your time,' she assured his huskily. 'Shani always gets what she wants, and anyway, if the attraction she holds for you is so strong, why fight it?'

His dark head jerked up and for a moment she thought he was about to contradict, but then shutters closed over his eyes and his silent withdrawal was assurance, if she had needed it, that he was acknowledging the truth of her words. Desperation gave her strength. Grabbing her handbag, she jumped to her feet and ran from the restaurant into the streets where jostling, happy crowds were following a parade of decorated floats. Beating drums and tambourines drowned her sobs, while the contagion of dancing fever and the warmth of the people helped by swallowing her up into a 'snake parade' that hid her from the tall dark figure she glimpsed emerging from the restaurant just seconds before she was swept out of sight.

CHAPTER FIVE

Hours later Lucille arrived back to the ship weary and dispirited, longing only for the solitude of her cabin wherein she might rest her fevered body and mind. She crept on tiptoe along the alleyway and had the key half turned in the lock of her cabin door when a hovering steward swooped. 'Miss Sharon wants to see you in her cabin, Miss Lamb.' Then with a pitying look, 'She's been anticipating your arrival for quite some time.' Used as he was to the tantrums of the wealthy and famous, his sympathy was aroused on behalf of a fellow sufferer whose large grey eyes registered desolation when she heard his news. For a second her body tensed, seemingly poised for flight, then a thin sigh foretold her surrender.

'Thank you,' she managed a tired smile. 'I'll tell Miss Sharon you passed on the message.' Her feet began to drag as she approached Shani's suite. She could hear a voice pitched high with anger coming from inside, followed by a deep-toned masculine one attempting to soothe. Her spirits rose. Art was inside with Shani; at least she could rely upon *his* support.

Her light tap upon the door must have gone unnoticed, because when she stepped inside neither Art nor Shani seemed aware of her entrance. Pacing with her back to the door, Shani was holding forth with such force that ice jangled madly inside the glass held in her posturing hand. 'This is the absolute end, I'm determined that this time she'll go!'

Art held his usual relaxed state, draping an armchair, but his tone was tight as he countered, 'Why, for heaven's sake? She's done nothing wrong. All right!' he held up a hand to ward off Shani's furious reply, 'according to the steward Lucille and Tareq went ashore together, but Tareq must have issued the invitation in the first place or she would never have gone. You can't possibly dismiss her for carrying out your instructions, which were—if you need reminding—to carry out whatever duties he demanded of her!'

'I might have expected you to speak up on her behalf,' she sneered. 'You're already halfway to being in love with the meek little madam yourself! But you don't know her as well as I do. That innocent bewilderment has fooled better men than you, even my own father—But enough about that, it's Tareq I'm concerned about. How dared he make excuses not to accompany me to Rio, then allow himself to be cajoled into escorting my secretary as soon as my back was turned!'

'Oh, no! ... I didn't ... It wasn't at all like that!' As Lucille's shocked whisper filled the angry silence two pairs of eyes swivelled in her direction. She flinched from Shani's thrust of venom and appealed wordlessly to Art, who responded by rising to his feet to hasten to her side.

'Just one minute, Art!' Shani commanded, digging iced-silver fingernails into his sleeve. 'Let's get one thing straight before emotion is allowed to overtake reason. Lucille is employed by me, I hired her and I'll fire her if I want to. If you interfere in any way I shall return home immediately and sue both you and the film company for loss of earnings brought about by your unwarranted intrusion into my personal affairs! Do I make myself clear?' she menaced softly, her hard glance daring him to transgress.

They were never to know what Art would finally have decided, because even as he hesitated, with both pairs of eyes scanning his worried face, a voice snapped the taut atmosphere with the amused observation, 'So you could not wait for me to join you before acquainting them with our news, *mon coeur*! Such astonished faces! Is it so surprising that I should have asked Lucille to become my wife?'

Never would Lucille have believed herself capable of feeling relief at the sound of Tareq's voice, nor so unbelievably comforted by the grip upon her waist that warned her to remain silent and leave the resolving of the nightmare situation to him. Strength drained out of her as she was hugged against his broad shoulder and her look of gratitude was returned with a glance so possessive it brought colour to her cheeks and incredulous disbelief to Shani's watchful eyes.

'What are you saying?' she rasped, shocked almost speechless by his whimsical confession.

His answer was physical. A thunderbolt could not have had more impact than the light kiss he feathered against Lucille's downcast lids, arousing vibrant trembling in a body aroused by his touch. She strove to hear his reply, muffled by the pounding in her ears.

'I am saying, dear Shani, that you and Art may be the first to congratulate me. I have found my ideal, the woman whose image I have carried in my heart for a lifetime! Truthfully, I had begun to doubt if the reality could exist, such sweetness, such purity, such rare understanding. These attributes are not given to many—and I have you, Shani, to thank for bringing us together. For that, I will remember you always with gratitude and pleasure.'

Lucille closed her eyes to shut out signs of battle warring across Shani's face. Tareq could be cruel, but did he have to be quite so callously indifferent when inflicting hurt? For the first time in her life she felt Shani deserved pity.

But obviously Art did not, and relief and triumph surged through his voice as he exclaimed, 'I'm delighted for you both, absolutely delighted! And your timing is perfect, Tareq. Only seconds before you arrived Shani had very reluctantly forced herself to dispense with Lucille's services.' Sarcasm laced his words as he challenged the temperamental star, 'Now you'll be spared the expense of Lucille's return flight, for I'm certain Tareq will insist upon having his fiancée close at hand while he's filming.'

Lucille sensed that Art had deliberately brought up the subject of the film in order to test out Shani's reaction, to find out whether the news she had just heard had piqued her to the extent of precipitating a refusal to continue working with Tareq. For anxious seconds her expression betrayed an urge to do just that, but she was nothing if not ambitious, and as co-starring with Tareq meant the furthering of her career common sense prevailed. Art had never admired her talents more than when she moved forward to kiss Lucille and to murmur, 'Congratulations, darling. I only hope you'll be capable of coping with this outrageous male who once publicly stated his opinion that women are born merely to obey the husband, to obey the father, and to obey the son ... !'

Late though it was, Tareq insisted upon adjourning to the One Deck Bar where he ordered champagne for everyone present. It was as if he intended the news of their bogus engagement to be spread far and wide in the shortest possible time, Lucille thought resentfully, as she accepted with as much grace as possible the hearty good wishes pressed upon her from all sides. The bar was a favourite haunt of the younger element aboard, its futuristic décor of chrome-swivel chairs, colourful leather upholstery and modern art forms satisfying their aspirations towards the stylish and the sophisticated. She felt immature and completely out of place at the side of the man who parried with ease the knowing looks and clever remarks being bandied from one to another of the dilettantes drunk with the excitement of being permitted close proximity to the élite social circle they had admired from afar.

Shani too was behaving well, bestowing gracious condescension upon the many fans whose conversation, liberally laced with flattery, could have been responsible for the flags of high colour in her cheeks and the extra bright sparkle in her eyes. Only Art was not deceived. Reaching Lucille's side during an interval when Tareq's attention was diverted by a girl intent upon discussion, he murmured the warning, 'Don't let Shani's supposed acceptance of the engagement fool you, princess. Underneath she's furious—and therefore dangerous!'

Lucille turned to him with relief, anxious to

explain how the misunderstanding had occurred and how angry she felt about Tareq's insistence upon publicising the impossible situation, but even as she began forming the first impulsive words Tareq swung round with a look so forbidding that the compulsion died.

'You look pale, *chérie*,' he offered smoothly. 'Let us seek some air.' Ignoring her obvious wish to remain with Art, he propelled her through the crowd, shrugging off with a cheerful grin the ribald comments of those who had surmised that they were anxious to be alone, and kept his grip firmly upon her waist until they reached the boat deck where secluded corners in deep shadow offered an obvious choice to lovers. Lucille felt marooned, cut off from civilization by a sky of black diamond-starred velvet and an unyielding ship's rail which was all that separated her from fathoms of sea racing and pounding as erratically as her own undisciplined heart. She pressed back against the rail, putting as much space as possible between herself and the dark shape towering above. He was a mere breath away, so relaxed that even through the darkness he projected amusement. She felt foolish when he mocked. 'Be calm, *ma petite*—here, there is no audience waiting for me to demonstrate my affection!' Nevertheless, when his hands reached out to cup the contours of her face his advice was rendered worthless.

'Why ... why did you involve me in this ridiculous farce?' she stammered, her face scorching his palms. 'Sooner or later Shani will discover the hold she has over you, then, however much you value your freedom, you'll be forced to give in.'

She was shocked by the sudden harshness of his

reply. 'A man cherishes two things, *chérie*, his freedom and his beloved. Usually he has to forgo one to keep the other, but this way I hope to retain both.'

'You mean Shani won't expect marriage while she thinks you are tied to me?' she faltered.

'*Juste*! And yet the lure of the unattainable is such that she will never cease to try. So you see, *ma petite*, with you as my gentle protector I cannot lose!'

Contempt made her trembled reply barely coherent. 'How dare you involve me in such cold-blooded deception! I told you in Rio that I wanted no part in such a scheme, yet you ignored my wishes and deliberately spread the news of our so-called engagement. Well, I'm sorry, *monsieur*, you may be made to look a little foolish when you announce the ending of the shortest betrothal on record, but if you don't do so immediately I will, right now, this very minute . . . !' She made to push past him, but was held rock-firm against his chest. Beneath her cheek she could feel his heart lifting and falling evenly, and the comparison with her own feeling of upheaval was humiliating.

'Have you forgotten that you, too, will benefit by allowing the engagement to stand?' he insinuated against her ear. 'Seconds before I announced my presence in her suite this evening I heard Shani dismiss you from your job. As my fiancée, you could enjoy a leisurely holiday in Egypt, quite properly financed by me, but what awaits you in England? Have you a home . . . money . . . another job?'

Lucille became very still. Bleakly, she was remembering how imperative it was that she should reach Egypt, how her whole future independence was reliant upon being able to research the final chapter of her book.

'Well, gentle Lucy?' he urged. 'The line of life runs raggedly between duty and desire, so why not overrule your scruples just this once and give way to the small wickedness of self-indulgence?'

She wavered under the spell of his silver tongue; it would be so easy to appease an awkward conscience with the reminder that the deception would harm no one. But the principle of honesty had been too well taught and after agonized seconds she knew what she had to do.

'I'm sorry,' she stated firmly, 'I couldn't possibly live such a lie, you'll have to find some other means of achieving your end.'

A muffled oath was his immediate answer, then his hands tightened to administer an aggravated shake. Frustration seethed in his voice as he clamped, 'Very well, you leave me no choice but to employ the only other means of persuasion left to me. I have noticed a strong attachment between yourself and Art. How much does his well-being mean to you?' Allowing her time for only a gasp of surprise, he raced on forcibly, 'If you refuse to do as I ask, then I shall make things awkward for your friend by refusing to carry out my contract! I need hardly spell out what that will mean ... the answers he will have to find for his film bosses if I should refuse to work with him! Remember also that we actors are imitative creatures,' he impressed cruelly, 'and what one does today the rest will do tomorrow!'

She could hardly believe he meant what he said; scanning his devil darkness she appealed: 'You're surely not threatening to ruin Art simply to get

59

your own way! Not even you could——' But he could and would. Something about his erect frame, about the agonizing grip digging into the soft flesh of her shoulders, told her he had never been more serious. Art, kind, loving Art, was to be sacrificed on the altar of one man's selfishness! When a soft moan escaped her he knew he had won, but she was too shocked and bewildered to notice that as he escorted her back to her cabin his stride though firm held none of the pride of victory.

The first departing members were emerging from the party just as they reached the entrance to the bar. Light from an open doorway spilled into the darkness, and mere seconds before Lucille spotted the revellers Tareq pulled up sharply and, whipping an arm around her waist, imprisoned her between himself and the ship's rail. His head swooped down and compelling lips stamped silence upon her protesting mouth with a kiss so prolonged she became storm-tossed, cast adrift upon heaving seas. With the skill of a professional he played out a love scene for the benefit of his audience, caressing with mounting passion the soft young body helplessly clinging to the only form of solidity left existing in a suddenly crazy world. Competently his fingers traced along her spine and he growled a throaty laugh when her fingers tightened convulsively upon the lapels of his jacket. Relishing his obvious power, he pressed her closer until their bodies fused into one, then bent her slowly backward until her slender body was draped bonelessly across his steel forearm. Lucille was incapable of physical resistance, and her breathless gasps for mercy went ignored as his lips sought and found the

60

virginal hollows of a young throat unused to the expertise of a professional lover. Practising every skill at his command, Tareq stirred into life every aching nerve, every pulsating sensation possible to newly awakened emotions until she began responding with insane abandon to every finger-light stroke, every featherweight touch of his lips.

She blushed to the fingertips when with all the fervour of a demented male he whispered. '*Mon petit agnelet*, how adorable it would be to love you—and to teach you to love!' She responded by shyly reaching up to stroke the lean plane of his cheek and alarmed laughter fluttered in her throat when he growled and made to pounce upon her fingers with white, even teeth. Her hasty withdrawal amused him, her timidity flattering his masterful ego, and encouraging him to tease her further.

'You are afraid of me!' he taunted. 'What must I do to convince you that far from the brutish, womanizing image my public relations people have worked hard to establish I am really a lonely male searching for a mate?'

'*You* lonely . . . ?'

'Is that so unusual?' he returned quickly. 'Half the world is looking for the other half, buyers for sellers, crooks for suckers, men for women . . .' His teasing note had completely gone and there in the darkness his words sounded sincere. Impulsively she raised her face, wanting to express sympathy and understanding with a kiss, and he accepted with a gentleness so profound she was moved almost to tears.

'*Bravo, bravo*! A superlative performance, Tareq!' The enthusiastic applause of an unseen audience reacted upon Lucille like a slap across the face. Furiously, she tore out of his arms, condemning with one stricken, horrified look his deplorable trickery before fleeing in the direction of her cabin, scarred to the heart by the knowledge that the tender interlude had been to him no more than a game, a not-to-be-missed opportunity of setting a seal upon their engagement by providing evidence for those who might have doubted its validity.

When she reached her cabin she threw herself on the bed until her breathing regained some form of normality. Her throat was aching with tears of shame and humiliation and as her mind raced back across the degrading incident a slow burning anger was born. '*Mon petit agnelet*!' he had whispered. My little lambkin! A hot blush scorched her skin. How naïve, how incredibly gullible he must have thought her, and yet how deserving she was of his derision. On principle, she loathed him, yet as had been so capably demonstrated, it took but the touch of his fingertips to send her nerves fleeing into an emotional panic. She moaned, then turned to bury flushed cheeks amongst cool sheets. She had to fight, had to rid herself of the plague the man had become!

In time, her body relaxed and she rolled over, reaching a decision. 'Very well, Monsieur Hawke, I'll join in your game! I'll even allow you to use me as a smoke-screen, but in return *I* shall use *you* as a means of reaching Egypt and after that as a means of staying there—so be prepared, my friend, to embark upon the most unrewarding gamble of your life!'

CHAPTER SIX

A WEEK later they disembarked at Cape Town in order to expedite the journey to Cairo. It was a wrench leaving the luxurious cruise ship, but Art was impatient to reach location and as the half-way-round-the-world cruise had been a great concession even Shani dared not demur when faced with the prospect of leaving behind the exquisite comfort of the greatest ship in the world for the less leisurely pace of a journey by air.

Conveniently, Shani had overlooked Lucille's peremptory dismissal and for the past week had dictated orders each morning as usual before sweeping off to enjoy whatever the day had in store. Lucille had not minded having an excuse to avoid Tareq, for since the morning after that fateful night, when she had sought him out to acquaint him of her decision, he had been off-hand to the point of curtness. She had gone as usual to his cabin, but had not been allowed to take dictation. 'There is a secretarial service aboard for the benefit of any passenger who might need one,' he had frowned when she had appeared, notebook in hand. 'If our engagement is to appear convincing you must abandon such duties and concentrate your attention upon me.'

She had swallowed hard, knowing that underlying the suggestion was a question waiting patently to be answered. 'I . . . will do as you ask, for the time being,' she had gasped, longing for a modicum of *savoir-faire* with which to acquaint him of her decision coolly and with perhaps a hint of scorn. But he, it seemed, had cornered the market in the quality of command she yearned.

'Good!' He had dismissed her all-important news and returned his attention to the letter he had thrust into the pocket of his dressing-gown the moment she had entered. After that one curt syllable there had seemed no reason to linger. For a few seconds Lucille had remained, shuffling from one foot to the other in embarrassed silence, but he had continued reading, too oblivious of her stumbling retreat to make any effort to detain her. From then on indignation had ruled her actions. Perversely, she had sought reasons not to appear in the dining-room or anywhere else he might by chance have been, but the expected rebuke had not been forthcoming, so her first week as the fiancée of one of the world's most eligible males had been spent in almost entire seclusion. Naturally, Shani had been quick to notice, and her satisfaction had registered in the arrogant issuing of orders calculated to reduce Lucille to the ranks she had so fleetingly abandoned.

They were being ushered towards their waiting aircraft when Shani decided to be awkward. 'Lucille, I've left my magazine in the transit lounge. Go back for it, please, it contains an article I particularly want to read.'

Lucille hesitated. The plane was warming up on the runway and the air hostess to whose flock they belonged seemed particularly anxious to avoid delay.

'Do you think I should?' she appealed. 'It's a

long way back and it might take ages to find. I'll get you another copy in Cairo,' she promised rashly. 'Such a popular magazine is sure to be available there.'

Shani stopped in her tracks. 'I want it now!' she demanded. 'The flight will be boring enough without something interesting to read.'

Casting a desperate glance at the expanse of concrete between herself and the airport buildings, Lucille wavered. She and Shani were at the rear of the crocodile of passengers, so if she sprinted she might just manage to make it back before the plane was ready for take-off. 'Very well,' she began to run, calling back across her shoulder, 'but don't let them take off without me!'

Her lungs felt ready for bursting by the time she reached the lounge; she leant against a wall for agonizing seconds before beginning a search for the mislaid magazine. Passengers for the next scheduled flight were already milling around the seats Shani and her party had vacated, and after five minutes' frantic questioning and apologising the magazine was at last located beneath the ample frame of an elderly gentleman who had almost to be heaved from his seat. 'Thank you so much ... so sorry to have been a nuisance ... I'm very grateful ...' Nagged by the necessity for speed, Lucille turned to run and in her haste collided with an object so solid she was rocked on her heels. Twin grips of steel fastened one on each elbow and through a red mist she heard the furious exclamation:

'Quelle témerité! Will you never learn!' To underline his annoyance Tareq shook her hard before whipping an arm around her waist to rush her back to the plane. Breathlessly she clung to him as he propelled her forward so fast the tips of her toes barely made contact with the ground. An anxious hostess ushered them inside the plane, then hovered only long enough to ensure that their seat belts were fastened before signalling that all was ready for take-off.

Power thrusting through metal, breathtaking speed, then the moment of lift-off when there is a feeling that one has left something of oneself behind, all these were secondary sensations to those engendered by Tareq's furious annoyance. Next to Lucille he sat silent, registering a severity disproportionate to her very minor crime. The worst that could have happened, she reflected with stubbornly held chin, was that she might have been left behind. But there were later flights and she was not so incompetent that she needed chaperoning during the few hours elapsing between flights. Under lowered lids she peeped up at him and was disconcerted to be caught out.

'Is this the object you considered of such great importance?' he derided, flicking the magazine she was clutching in a tight fist.

Avoiding the glint that seemed to spell out trouble, she tried to explain, 'Shani insisted——'

'In future, any insisting that has to be done, I will do!' he stated without apology for interrupting. Lucille blinked. 'Aboard ship your regrettable tendency to avoid my company could be overlooked, but in Cairo where I and my family are well known it would be as well if you were seen often to defer to my wishes and to act out as competently as you are able the rôle of a girl happily betrothed to the man she loves. Your acting ability will be gravely taxed, I know, but my own skill in that direction should help to cover up any glaring deficiencies.'

It seemed stiflingly hot in the aircraft, especially when his sleeve brushed against her arm, bringing tingling warmth. Memories of his last demonstration of acting skill returned to torment her. 'Of that I have no doubt!' The words escaped sounding like a condemnation. She quivered, expecting a cutting reply, but her heart missed a beat when instead of deriding Tareq hesitated as if considering an explanation. But then he shrugged, leant back his head, and closed his eyes to shut from sight her unhappy face with eyes reminiscent of a locked-out kitten left shivering to contemplate its fate.

Cairo, though the oldest of cities, looked surprisingly modern. Luxury skyscraper hotels reflected startlingly white in the deep waters of the Nile, the city's main thoroughfare upon which surface water buses skimmed, churning long lines of glistening spray in their wakes. High-powered cars darted amongst the buses and taxis crossing many low-slung bridges, and soaring above rounded minarets and angular buildings was a concrete tower with an attractive open lattice-work covering that gave to the obelisk-like structure an appearance of deceptive fragility.

Lucille's disappointed expression drew a consoling observation from Tareq. 'Do not judge too harshly the architects of modern civilization, *chérie*. The ancient parts of the city have been carefully preserved, indeed so many mosques abound that it is said that if a Moslem were to pray in a different one each day for a year he still would not enter all the mosques of Cairo.'

Her sigh of relief yielded from him an understanding smile. Their taxi was speeding through a commercial centre containing high blocks of flats, shops and banks divided by depressingly suburban, acacia-lined streets. They were heading towards the hotel which was to accommodate members of the film company until arrangements for the planned move to a location somewhere in the desert had been finalized.

'I must see the Pyramids and the Sphinx, and——'

'I'll take you tonight,' he indulged her negligently.

'In the dark ... ?' she asked hesitantly, anxious for the experience but wary of missing a single thing.

'We can return in daylight, if you wish,' he conceded, 'but after this evening I feel sure you will agree there is no more rewarding sight than the Pyramids at night. Trust me,' he reached out to give her an avuncular pat. 'This city was once my home, so who should know better which are the choicest plums in this particular pie?'

Shani was most displeased not to have been invited. She barged into the bedroom while Lucille was dressing and all the spleen pent up inside her since the announcement of the engagement was released at the sight of her cousin's flushed cheeks and air of excited anticipation.

'Where are you off to, pray?' she probed coldly, her eyes questioning the suitability of Lucille's dress and the matching light wool coat draped upon the bed. She was herself wearing an evening gown of golden organza, the bodice boned to cup the curve of her breasts and leaving tempting shoulders bare —an outfit most suitable for dining in the cosmopolitan, highly exclusive hotel.

Lucille's muscles reacted with a spasm to the hostile question. As usual, in Shani's company she felt inadequate and very conscious of the deceit she was being forced to practise. 'Tareq and I are dining out,' she faltered, then soldiered on, very conscious of an embarrassed blush. 'He's taking me to see the Pyramids by moonlight.'

Shani prowled forward with the stealth of a cat and Lucille backed nervously away. Stripped of defence, she quivered under the glare of her visibly aggravated inquisitor and fear chased through her when Shani condemned, 'There's something unconvincing about this engagement of yours. For one thing, it was too sudden, and for another—I believe you're actually terrified of him!' she hissed so malevolently that Lucille jumped. Cornered, she could do no more than stare back at her attacker while expressions of doubt, shame and bewilderment chased across her features. She wanted to deny the accusation, but could not find the words, and even if she had, instinct told her Shani would have enjoyed ripping to pieces any fabrication of lies.

Only mere seconds before confession was wrung from her a rap on the door heralded salvation. Ignoring Shani's snapped order to pay it no attention, Lucille ran past and almost fell into Tareq's arms as he crossed the threshold. A glance across her shoulder offered all the clues needed to explain her wide-eyed distress and the relief with which she had flown into arms that had opened instinctively to receive her.

'Are you ready, *chérie*?' His voice was as calming as the pressure of his arms. Lucille lifted up her face, meaning to nod, but to her horror tears spurted. Quick to react, he bent his head and tenderly kissed them away, the brush of his cool lips encouraging assurance upon glistening lashes and fluttering eyelids so that with regained confidence she was able to turn in his arms to bestow upon Shani a shaky smile.

'I'm sorry, Shani, I've quite forgotten. What was it you asked?' she uttered on a short breath. Lucille alone was one thing, but Lucille fortified by Tareq's dominating presence was quite another. As Shani left, sweeping aside the question with an angry wave, Lucille shivered, convinced that the inquisition she had so neatly side-stepped had not been abandoned but was merely postponed.

Cairo's night sky was ablaze with light when Tareq escorted her down the steps of the hotel towards a waiting taxi. She hesitated, casting a wistful look across her shoulder to where a fountain surrounding an illuminated statue of Rameses the Second invited further investigation. On impulse, she pleaded, 'Couldn't we walk a little of the way? There's so much I'd like to see and so little time ...'

Raised eyebrows, indicative of surprise, were engulfed by a frown as Tareq considered her request. He seldom walked in public places, past experience having taught him that the best defence against the invasion of privacy was a swift, unobtrusive limousine. But her appealing and obvious excitement could not be denied. 'Very well,' his expressive shrug won a sympathetic grin from the taxi driver who was instructed, 'Pick us up in an hour on the south side of Liberation Square.'

The stolen hour was both a victory and a delight. As her enthusiasm was communicated to him his reserve began to slip and for the second half hour he was a boy again, exploring anew the city of Arabian Nights. With pointing finger he indicated sights she might have missed; donkey boys tending their beasts on the river banks; a sad-faced Bisharin boy, short and slight, dressed in the age-old manner of his people; feluccas resting in the lee of bridges, and others, their cream sails bellying in the breeze, gliding along the water.

In the oldest part of the city they stood amongst a crowd of Arabs being entertained by a *gulli-gulli* man, a street conjuror whose sleight of hand impressed Lucille far more than the rest of his audience who seemed for the most part to have guessed how his tricks were achieved. During one part of their journey Tareq took hold of her hand to prevent their becoming separated, but she became conscious of the intimacy only when in a moment of excitement she tugged him to a halt in front of a house that had survived the passing of many centuries. Its brick façade was crumbling, but what had taken her eye was the ancient Mushrabia screens fastened around the windows of what had evidently been the women's quarters—screens through which the womenfolk of the family might see yet remain unseen.

'How totally primitive!' she whispered, then on a shaky breath, 'And how pitifully deprived those poor creatures must have been.'

'I do not agree!' he crisped, rising against the implied criticism. 'We respect our women and treat them well. Would they not revolt against us if we did not?'

Wide-eyed, Lucille searched his hawk-like features. *We* respect ... *we* treat ... There in the narrow, shadowy side street she was reminded forcibly of his claim to Arab blood, of the pride and whispered nobility of his mother's race. He lacked nothing, neither arrogance nor strength, to debar his recognition from a lineage as proud and as ancient as the Pharaoh's! It was an effort to remember that they were existing in the twentieth century; at that moment he seemed capable of sweeping her off her feet to deposit her within the confines of a jealously guarded harem, to reflect upon her transgressions and then possibly, when she was properly repentant, to await his pleasure!

She forced a nervous laugh. 'Are you suggesting that Eastern women enjoyed the purdah imposed upon them by despotic males? If so, why have so many of them rejected such practice by claiming for themselves a greater share of public life and equality with their menfolk? No, *monsieur*, today's women would react violently against the wearing of the veil!'

As if to confound her theory, a figure glided from out of a nearby doorway draped from head to foot in flowing white robes, a yashmak concealing the lower half of her face leaving uncovered only an inch of brow rising above modestly downcast eyes. Nodding towards the retreating girl, Tareq countered, 'I find such modesty delightful. Emancipated women scavenge a man's emotions—who would not exchange a raven for a dove?'

He was referring, of course, to the attentions he

received from his many women admirers, unwelcome and unsought attentions suffered as the price of fame but inwardly despised by this man whose thoughts and actions were influenced by a lusty arrogance inherited from ancestors whose roots sprang deeply from wild, untameable desert. Lucille lapsed into silence, regretting the impulsive argument that had chased carefree happiness and left frowning displeasure in its place.

The drive out to the Pyramids, which took no more than twenty minutes, was accomplished in complete silence. Uneasily, she noted his brooding expression and yearned for a return of the companionship she had earlier enjoyed, but as they drove along the modern highway away from the heart of Cairo he seemed absorbed in deep and singular thought.

Her first sight of the Pyramids was an unexpected one. Suddenly, the built-up area ceased and there, on a high plateau, were the great mountains of stone. From then onwards she was no longer conscious of his silence; words would have been superfluous anyway as they toured the immense bases, feeling the roughness of centuries-old stone beneath her hand as tentatively she stroked the colossal sides and gazed with wonder at the inscrutable Sphinx stretched out on guard at the foot of the ancient mounds. Later, they watched as in an open-air theatre five thousand years of splendid past was portrayed against a backcloth of vast monuments picked out of the darkness by coloured searchlights. Crickets chattering in the background and a desert dog barking far away in the sands barely penetrated her absorption, so that when the lights faded and the music died she was left feeling bemused and even a little deprived.

As Tareq guided her back to the taxi she was grateful that he made no attempt to break the spell. Heart and mind were still captured within the past, reluctant to abandon the compelling enticement of a long-dead era momentarily resurrected. Once back at the hotel, however, she surfaced long enough to thank him as they lingered outside her bedroom door. She was fumbling with her key when his fingers closed around hers to direct the key towards the lock. He leant so close her lashes brushed his cheek and the contact made her shy.

'Thank you for allowing me to share such a glorious experience, Tareq,' she breathed, still full of wonder. A fractional movement of his head brought his lips level with hers and instinctively she moved so that their lips touched in a kiss of fleeting sweetness.

It was all a part of the magic of the night, she told herself as she prepared for bed. Leaping pulses, the sensation of walking inches from the ground, even the wayward trembling of her limbs had been brought about by the excitement of a unique performance and were definitely not the result of the avuncular kiss bestowed so absently her lips could have been those of a grateful child. But her feelings were far from childlike as she snapped out the light and snuggled down to sleep . . . to dream of ancient Pharaohs whose divine and royal features bore a disturbing resemblance to the vital, flesh-and-blood man whose contradictory attitudes left her floundering in a confused morass of love and hate.

CHAPTER SEVEN

DURING the days that followed Lucille became aware that Tareq's reputation as a professional charmer was not undeserved. For reasons of his own he reversed the procedure by switching his attentions to Shani, leaving Lucille to gather the remaining crumbs of his time. In retrospect, the motive behind his manoeuvre was not hard to find; by his own admission he intended bending Shani's will to his and, skilled tactician that he was, he had planned to achieve such dominance first of all by pretending interest in another, then, with masterly knowledge of his subject, proceeding to bombard his prey with attentions guaranteed to turn the head of any woman, much less Shani who, for all her bravado, was surprisingly susceptible to his appeal.

'*Egotistical beast!*' Lucille fumed, painfully aware of the rôle she had been allocated, and determined, now the blinkers had been removed, that he would never find her so malleable again.

They were draped in various poses around the hotel swimming pool. Shani, in a vivid green swim-suit, was stretched out on a sun-lounger, her eyes caressing Tareq who was lying at the edge of the pool splashing the water with his feet and watching with aesthetic interest sunlight endowing each separate drop with the clarity of rainbow crystal. Art was progressing with slow, powerful strokes along the length of the pool and as he approached he appealed to Lucille:

'Come on in, lazybones, the water's lovely but lonely!' As he trod water his appreciative eyes roamed her slender figure outlined by a black swimsuit contrasting starkly against white-blonde hair, its simple lines even more exciting to the eye than the exotic creation barely pretending to cover Shani.

'I could jump in and be drowned for all they'd notice!' Lucille fumed when neither companion evinced the slightest interest. It was a relief to dive into the temper-cooling water, but as she struck out towards Art she was conscious that Tareq's dark head had not swerved even fractionally in her direction.

She was angry with herself for feeling so ridiculously aggrieved. He had made no attempt at denial when she had accused him of using their bogus engagement as a shield against the attraction he felt for Shani. A shallow, lighthearted affair was all he intended; deeper lasting relationships were as superfluous to him as they were to prowling desert predators, loners that mated at will, then resumed their solitary way. *Mon aimable protectrice!* he sometimes mocked her. At that moment Lucille felt incapable of being either gentle or protective!

When Art swam to meet her he received a delightful smile of welcome, and immediately his expression lightened. He, too, had been worried by Tareq's incomprehensible preference for Shani's company, but if Lucille did not mind then it followed that he had little cause for worry. As a producer, used to artifice, he should have recognized acting, but as they frolicked together in the water, their teasing, diving, surfacing accompanied by much carefree laughter, her heaviness of heart was so skilfully disguised he never once suspected that Tareq's brooding presence was uppermost in her mind.

He was watching them through eyes narrowed against the glare of the sun. Certainly, annoyance could hardly have been responsible for brows knitted so severely that they met in a straight forbidding line. To Art's astonishment Lucille developed a sudden urge to torment. Flashing through the water like a slender shadow, she caught him a blow behind the knees, causing him to flounder, then before he could regain his breath she appeared beside him and with the flat of her hand pushed his head beneath the surface. Laughter turned to screams of panic when he recovered sufficiently to begin to retaliate. Kicking up a flurry of spray, she set off up the pool with Art following closely, set upon revenge. As his more powerful strokes narrowed the gap between them he reached out to grab her ankles and they went down together, arms and legs tangling as they threshed water. They surfaced spluttering, helpless with laughter, Lucille's eyes sparkling with the reflected blue of sky and water, her hair a cap of gold plastered around a face alive with enjoyment.

A cloud crossed the sun, and at that precise moment a voice intruded coldly, 'Someone wishes to speak with you on the telephone, Art; as the matter is urgent the caller preferred to wait rather than ring back later.'

'Thanks, Tareq!' Art grinned, but before leaving the pool he threatened darkly, 'As for you, young woman, be prepared for punishment when I get back!'

Tareq had joined them in the deep end and as Art clambered up the steps Lucille turned to follow, feeling suddenly chilled. But Tareq had no intention of being left alone, as the tight grip he fastened around her waist forcibly intimated.

'Well, little minnow, have you no sparkle left for me? See, look around at all the interested spectators asking themselves why a woman who shines so much in the company of one man should display cold indifference to the presence of her betrothed!' His smile was a white-toothed replica of those he reserved for the cameras, but his eyes betrayed anger only she could see. To her embarrassment she saw a crowd had gathered around the pool, and judging from the expressions of amusement it was expected that Tareq should continue where Art had left off.

'I'm c-cold ...' she appealed through chattering teeth, not really expecting him to believe her when water was caressing their bodies like warm milk.

'Then float and look adoringly into my eyes,' he mocked. 'Our audience must not be disappointed.' But such pretence was beyond her. Who could tell what secrets he might probe from her expressive face if by chance acting should escalate into reality and her mask were allowed to slip?

'I can't ...'

'You must!' was his adamant reply. His grip upon her waist relaxed to allow her to float and like quicksilver she flashed through his hands, heading towards the steps. She reached them—her toes were actually curling around the first rung—when she was plucked up and pinioned against a muscled brown chest. She knew better than to resist. His

pride was aroused, an audience was waiting to be
entertained and his victory must be demonstrated!
A thudding sound impinged through her agitation.
It was her heart thumping against the wall of his
chest, a fragile battering ram reverberating through
her body. Then a stronger beat became noticeable
as his heart answered, rocking her breathless with
its message of power, of arrogance, of impenetrable
defences.

To the smiling crowd they must have appeared
deeply in love. Tareq's mouth was tender, his expression a mask of devotion as he gazed down at the
delicate wraith clinging around his neck as if she
never wanted to let go. Nor did she. Fearful of his
intentions, she wished to anticipate his actions so
that she might attempt a second, more successful
escape from the limelight she abhorred.

The finale came so suddenly she was completely
unprepared. One minute there was blue sky,
sparkling water, colourful sun umbrellas shading
groups of amused faces, then in the next Tareq's
dark head swooped across her vision as he bent to
crush her salt-tanged mouth with hard lips demanding fire in exchange for steel. Fire she had in plenty,
it ran liquid through her veins down to clutching
fingertips, to curling toes, to every innermost pulse
lain dormant up until this moment of violent awakening when the touch of his lips made mockery of
notions of timidity or lukewarm affection. Slowly
they sank under water, their bodies entwined, and
as they descended their lips clung ... and clung
further ...

Inwardly, bells were ringing, fireworks were ex-
ploding, and her senses felt wholly seduced by the

time they surfaced to gulp in air and to experience the shock of enthusiastic applause. This time he made no attempt to detain her when she struck out for the side and ran to hide scarlet cheeks from an appreciative crowd. Her crowning humiliation was a strident wolf whistle—its message unmistakable— that followed in her wake and seemed to reverberate in her head even hours later. She felt she had been stamped with the mark of the Hawk. No longer a girl, she was a woman—*his woman*—deliberately and publicly branded as a warning that in future he would tolerate no further involvement, however platonic, with any other man!

There was a brooding quality about Tareq's smile when later that evening she forced herself to appear in the bar where they had formed the habit of meeting for pre-dinner drinks. He and Shani seemed absorbed in conversation, but immediately Lucille entered his head swivelled in her direction as if instinctively aware of her presence. Her heart lifted, and as he moved towards her she sensed his complacent awareness of the turbulence he aroused beneath the high-necked bodice of cream lace whose creator had cleverly avoided a look of demureness by the use of skilful cutting. Each curve from shoulder to thigh was beautifully outlined as she drifted slowly forward, her features bearing a startling resemblance to the profile etched finely upon the cameo strung upon black velvet ribbon around her neck.

'I have never seen you looking more beautiful, *chérie*,' he assured her gravely as he took her hand to lead her forward.

Wild colour stung her cheeks. Once more the

devilish game had begun.

Shani, of course, was within earshot and was directing daggers of jealousy in her direction. 'I quite liked that dress myself,' she drawled. 'Indeed, I wore it so often I never imagined it would be fit to wear again once I'd discarded it! What a clever girl you are, Lucille.' Then with false generosity, 'There are some other dresses in my wardrobe for which I have no more use. I'll let you have them tomorrow.'

Lucille's mortification was not appeased by the sympathy that flashed into Tareq's eyes nor by the tightening pressure of fingers that threatened to crush the life out of her hand. Delicately, she disengaged his clasp and thanked Shani in a voice she would not allow to tremble. It would have been useless to try to fight back, her stumbling protest would have been annihilated by Shani's swift repartee, and as for Tareq, it must be suiting him well enough to have in his power a creature too timid and too lacking in spirit to revolt against even this most outrageous behaviour.

It was a credit to his acting ability that he should seem so sincerely anxious to assure himself of her comfort when he handed her into a chair and signalled to a passing waiter. 'What would you like to drink, *chérie*? Might I suggest you try something fairly innocuous which will combine harmlessly with the white wine I have ordered with our meal? It is called Cleopatra, and is brewed from vineyards on the self-same site as the wine which so pleased Mark Antony's palate. I especially want you to try it.'

She pleated the material of her skirt with nervous

fingers, wishing he would switch his bombardment of charm to Shani whose mouth was tightening ominously.

'Anything will do,' she husked, her troubled grey eyes unconsciously pleading to be allowed to resume her usual place in the background. Every eye was upon them, wondering, no doubt, why the savagely attractive, superbly assured actor should have chosen as his future bride the meek child whose pale features blurred into insignificance in comparison with the vital beauty of his other companion.

Art's arrival was a blessed relief, but as he strode into the bar and made towards their table worry and frustration were plainly evident. 'Order me a drink, will you, Tareq? A whisky and soda—make it a double!'

With raised eyebrows Tareq complied, then turned his attention back to Art, whose anxiety was so great he was barely articulate as he rushed into explanation.

'The film's off! The location we had in mind has been put out of bounds by the medical authorities because of an outbreak of some disease thought to have been caused by contamination of the water.'

'But it must surely be just a localized quarantine?' Tareq frowned. 'Can't you find a similar spot in which to carry on filming?'

'That wouldn't be impossible,' Art's fingers tugged impatiently through his hair. 'All we require in the way of scenery is sand, space and a nearby oasis, but accommodation is our main problem. As you know, finding suitable quarters for all technicians, actors and camera crews is our biggest headache. Rooms have to be booked months in advance, which means that, although another location would be easy to find, there's no place within a hundred miles where an outfit of our size could be accommodated at such short notice.'

'Oh, damnation!' Shani's expression put the blame squarely on Art's shoulders. 'What a waste of time and money!'

'You'll be paid,' Art retorted sourly.

'How?' she flashed back. 'People in our profession must remain constantly in the public eye, and how do we do that if we're not filming? A few measly pounds will hardly recompense for the dwindling interest of thousands of fans!'

Art winced, knowing that what she said was true. Nothing was more fickle than an audience deprived of contact with its idols. Shani's star was rising, but she had not yet reached the height of popularity enjoyed by such as Tareq, who was such a firmly entrenched favourite that his absence would merely whet his public's appetite, whereas Shani's might well go ignored.

Art's misery compelled comfort, and impulsively Lucille reached out to him. 'Don't worry, something will turn up, I'm sure of it!'

Quickly she withdrew her hand when Tareq's glance seared a warning and though she did not meet his eyes she felt his look was upon her when he drawled, 'The difficulty is not unsurmountable.' When Art's head jerked up, he continued slowly, 'Not far from here is an oasis where my mother has a house with rooms enough to shelter an army. Naturally, they are not all in use. My mother's apartments take up a very small amount of space and the rest has been allowed to fall into disuse.

However, servants are plentiful at the Oasis of Behdet, so in a matter of hours the rooms could be made habitable.' He paused to consider their reactions. Art's relief was obvious, as was Shani's delight, but Lucille's expression of near panic caused him to frown.

'Won't your mother mind having us descend upon her without warning?' Art questioned, hardly daring to believe his luck.

Tareq shook his head. 'No, her apartments are in the old harem quarters, cut off from the rest, and unless she should wish it, she need hardly be aware of your presence.'

'How exciting!' Shani radiated. 'It must be a very large and very ancient house?'

His lips curled into a smile. 'It is. The Palace of Horus is centuries old and has been in the possession of my mother's family since it was built. You'll find it a unique building, containing much that will appeal to the romantics in our midst.' It was no coincidence that his glance should swivel on to Lucille's bent head and linger as if fascinated on the nape of her neck where fine hairs had escaped their chignon and lay like strands of gold against its velvet softness. His voice when he addressed her direct was surprisingly tender. 'And what of you, *petit agnelet*—are you perhaps nervous of encroaching into the desert deep where primitive tribesmen are still insistent upon keeping their women in purdah?'

His indulgent mockery struck a spark between them and her chin lifted even though her mouth still retained an anxious quiver. 'Women are quite safe in the hands of desert tribesmen, *monsieur*.

84

They, I believe, are bound by a code of honour far stricter than any imposed upon men of the Western world. It is the civilized savage we women have most cause to fear. . . ! '

Shani's gasp of amusement was the only sound that impinged upon the silence. Art was staring open-mouthed, searching Lucille's white face for a clue to her uncharacteristic sharpness. Undoubtedly she was agitated, her clenched fists and rapid breathing told him so, but his puzzled eyes could not probe out the reason.

Lucille longed to be able to refuse. She was appalled at the idea of meeting and acting out a lie in the presence of Tareq's mother. Already, she had suffered agonies of conscience about their bogus engagement, and although an excursion into the desert with plenty of time for research was the sole reason behind her acceptance of the deception, she felt neither satisfaction nor triumph—merely shame on her own behalf and contempt for Tareq on account of his willingness to deceive his mother. But once again her scruples would have to be sacrificed for the sake of Art. Tareq had offered him a lifeline—she could not be the one to cut it!

That he was fully aware of her dilemma was made obvious by his mocking reply. 'I take it, then, that you are not afraid to venture into my desert domain, *mon ami*? Obviously, you consider a thousand untamed tribesmen will constitute less of a threat to your peace of mind than I who, I presume, am the civilized savage you spoke of! '

CHAPTER EIGHT

THE journey to the oasis took an exhausting twelve hours by car. At the beginning the desert road ran through fields, then it began sloping upwards as they neared the desert plateau. On either side of the road great oval-shaped rocks lay strewn amongst the sand, eroded by wind, some cracked open as if by the impact of a giant karate chop.

'The stones become overheated by the sun, then crack and split if there is an exceptionally cold night', Tareq explained to Lucille, whose determination to fight off drowsiness caused by heat and fatigue was betrayed by an occasional jerk and the forcing apart of eyelids that were threatening to obscure from sight interesting details.

She gazed around, wondering how people existed amidst such arid emptiness. The car was at the head of a large convoy of trucks laden with the equipment Art had adamantly refused to have sent by rail. Experience had taught him never to allow anything of importance out of his sight, so like an army on the move, everything necessary to their mission was being toted by the troops.

'How much farther, for heaven's sake?' Shani queried waspishly, dabbing perspiration from her top lip. Although the car Tareq was driving was the ultimate in luxury, after a few hundred miles its air-cooling system had begun to seem less and less efficient in the fight against waves of torrid heat and particles of ground dust that had somehow penetrated cracks between doors and windows.

'Watch closely, and soon you'll begin to see the first outlines of the oasis,' he nodded, indicating the horizon.

Lucille craned forward to scan the dunes. At first she could see nothing, then gradually, like a vast green ship in a sea of yellow sand, the oasis began to take shape. It was immense. Far larger than she had anticipated, it lay in a depression and stretched out fingers of lush greenery for dozens of miles. As they drew closer, what she had imagined as a ship's masthead turned out to be a minaret towering loftily above surrounding palm trees and nearer to earth acacia tamarisk, wild senna and fruit trees grew in profusion.

'Why the Palace of Horus?' Lucille asked suddenly. 'Does the name have any special significance?'

Her interest in everything ancient and unusual had not gone unnoticed by Tareq, and as it both intrigued and pleased him he never hesitated to slake her thirst for knowledge. 'Horus was an ancient Pharaonic god. During religious ceremonies priests would don animal masks when representing gods, because each god not only possessed all the virtues of a human but also a particular attribute from animal or bird. Sekmet, the god of war, had the strength of the lion, Anubis the fleetness of the jackal, and Horus the keen sight of the hawk.'

'Then it is the Palace of the Hawk?' she faltered, avoiding the keen look which warned that there were others who could claim affinity with the soaring hawk whose eye never flinched from the sun.

They continued on through lush date plantations and olive groves, then finally down a corridor of bare rock towards an ancient structure, its walls contrasting bronze against a cobalt blue sky. Instinct warned Lucille that this was the Palace of Horus, the place from which a beautiful princess had been wooed by the passionate courtship of a young French Army officer. Had it been a successful union? she wondered, then shivered as she glanced sideways at the offspring of the marriage. What possible mercy could be expected from a man descended from the House of Horus—the sharp-eyed hawk?

They entered a silent courtyard through an archway of carved stone depicting the outspread wings of the hawk god. A vast pillared hall beckoned with the promise of cool shade and then when they entered enthralled them with the beauty of a mosaic floor portraying scenes that leapt to vivid life beneath their feet. From out of the dusky background a servant appeared, white-robed, his impassive features bearing no sign of welcome nor even curiosity at the sight of a courtyard filling rapidly with an assortment of men and vehicles.

'If my mother has not yet retired for the night, Sobhi, ask one of her women to acquaint her with the news of my arrival.' A grin of recognition followed by a rapid spate of unintelligible words welcomed Tareq back into the fold and minutes later the hall was swarming with servants eager to serve their master and their master's friends.

Lucille found it sheer bliss to relax in a bath of petal-scented water, then to wander barefoot into her bedroom where a young Arab girl was absorbed in her task of unpacking her suitcases. She hesitated when Lucille entered, her shy eyes uncertain as she awaited further orders.

'Put down those things and talk to me,' Lucille urged, her fatigue completely gone. 'What is your name? Do you live here in the palace, or is your home in some other part of the oasis?'

'My name is Ashra, which means ten, because I am the tenth daughter of my father and mother,' the girl replied slowly in halting English. 'My sisters and I have lived here in the palace for many years, but sometimes we are allowed to visit my father's camp when he is away, to see our mother, who grieves for our company even though she knows we are well cared for in the service of the Princess. Of course, we always make sure that my father's eye does not fall upon us.'

Lucille lounged on the bed, her face a picture of interest. 'Why? Is there ill-feeling between yourselves and your father?'

'Ill-feeling ...?' Ashra, the tenth one, struggled to understand.

'Don't you like him—or doesn't *he* like you?' Lucille clarified.

'We love our father!' the girl answered with amazed politeness. 'It is simply that the sight of us is a reminder to him of his great misfortune. Truly, Allah greatly curses him who has no sons!'

Lucille jerked upright with surprise. 'You mean that you girls have become outcasts from society simply because your misguided father considers you to be of an inferior sex? *Diablo!*' unconsciously she imitated one of Tareq's milder imprecations, 'the man should be horsewhipped!' Ashra cowered away, her features crumbling, and Lucille realized with quick shame that her rapid words had not

89

been understood—only her anger had registered. She jumped from the bed and ran towards the shivering girl, still no more than a child, who flinched away from her outstretched hand as if expecting a blow. Lucille recoiled from the thought and quickly clasped her hands behind her as she pleaded, 'Don't be afraid, I'm not angry with *you*, only with the system that allows such discrimination—favouritism,' she substituted, remembering the girl's limited vocabulary. 'I would like to be your friend—I want you to be *my* friend! Please,' she brought her hand from behind her back and extended it slowly, 'let's shake on it?'

'Shake . . .?'

'Yes,' Lucille's emphatic nod loosened already insecure pins so that a silken coil of hair slid down across her shoulder. Its beauty added to the appeal of grey eyes dark with remorse and helped to sweep away any lingering doubts the girl might have been harbouring.

'Shake . . .' Slim brown fingers crept out to bestow a fleeting touch, then were shyly withdrawn, but not before a shared smile of understanding had put a seal upon the relationship.

'Thank you, Ashra.' Lucille expelled a relieved breath, then determined to sift thoroughly until she was in possession of all the facts she probed further. 'Tell me more about your circumstances. Are you happy here, do you ever wish you had access to places of learning such as are available in the cities?'

Ashra settled cross-legged on the floor and considered carefully. 'What is happiness?' she sighed. 'The Princess Samira does not have me beaten for small misdemeanours, I am well fed and my quarters are comfortable. I think I am happy ...' Her brows knit. 'I will know for certain after my wedding. Then my husband will be made known to me and the time of wondering will be over.'

Lucille could barely believe the words spoken with such fatalistic acceptance. 'What? Do you mean you are being made to marry a man you've never yet seen?'

Ashra seemed startled by the vehement question. 'But yes, it is customary not only for the preliminaries of marriage, but also for the ceremony itself to be performed in the absence of the bride. The proposal of marriage and the contract is carried out not by the bride and bridegroom but by their friends and sponsors, or parents. My father and my bridegroom's father will join hands, their hands will then be covered by a ceremonial cloth. A cup of wine will be shared and when they have both drunk from the cup the marriage is confirmed.'

'And it will be only then that you will see your bridegroom?' Lucille interrupted.

Ashra checked a nod, then half-smiled. 'Not quite,' her smile became a chuckle that incensed Lucille's curiosity to boiling point.

'When, then ...?' she urged, impatient of the girl's lack of independent spirit. Meek though she herself purported to be, nothing on earth could induce her to submit to such indignity.

'My father's tribe follow a rite which he insists must be incorporated into the marriage ceremony. On the evening before the day the marriage is to take place, the girl runs away into the hills and the bridegroom goes in search of her. When he has found her he stays the night with her, and once this is done there can be no turning back. Even if, for some reason, the ceremonial part of the wedding does not take place, in the eyes of their people they are irrevocably wed.'

'I don't believe it ...! Can't believe that in these enlightened days any place is remote enough from civilization to retain such barbaric practices!' But even as Lucille condemned she sensed she could be wrong. Here in this remote desert outpost life was being lived as it had been centuries ago, so much so that the sight of a Pharaonic procession wending its leisurely way through a path of prone, worshipping subjects would hardly have surprised her. She pinched herself as a reminder that she was existing within the twentieth century when all that remained of ancient Egypt was the debris of cities long buried under sand and rubble; temples and tombs dedicated to the eternal life and power of ancient gods and kings—and a handful of tribes who had resisted progress to the extent of clinging to outmoded and barbaric rites.

'You don't have to go through with it,' she declared impulsively. 'I'll speak to Tareq—he'll be as appalled as I am to learn that such impositions are still being suffered by the females of this community. I'll go right now in search of him to tell him he must put a stop to the wedding arrangements immediately!'

The smile around Ashra's lips faded as lashes swept down over eyes grown suddenly bleak. With one lithe movement she rose to her feet and stood with bent head before bowing her leave. 'May it be as you wish, my lady,' she intoned with such lack of enthusiasm Lucille was nonplussed.

'Don't you *want* to be released from a lifetime of bondage?' she faltered, sensing the girl's resentment.

'The Koran instructs our men: "Your women are your fields—go out into your fields at will". I do not wish to be regarded as an infertile, barren waste,' she muttered, rendering Lucille speechless ...

'My mother has retired for the night, but she has asked me to bid you welcome and to tell you she hopes to take tea with you tomorrow, some time in the afternoon. A servant will be sent to fetch you.' They were gathered together for dinner in one of the smaller downstairs rooms. When Tareq repeated his mother's request, Shani acknowledged the invitation with a pleased smile, but when Lucille remained deep in thought he strode towards her across an expanse of richly embroidered carpet. 'Well, what impression has the Palace of Horus stamped upon your susceptible mind?'

He knew she was still unaware of him when her attention remained fixed upon the unusually shaped alabaster jar she was examining. On the lid lay a lion, tongue lolling, its body smooth and cool to the touch, and on the sides were scenes showing lions and dogs hunting bulls and gazelles. Two side columns supported the lid and from the heavy base protruded four heads of prisoners, each bearing the agonized expression peculiar to those overburdened with weight. The jar held her mesmerized—it appealed as an indication of the savage contained within the sophisticate, a magnificent piece of workmanship lovingly carved out of priceless stone into an effigy so cruel it repelled.

Tareq's question was an intrusion; as she swung round to face him she coloured, wondering if thought association had spirited him to her side. 'What ... what did you say?'

'It doesn't matter,' he took an untouched goblet of wine from her hand and set it down upon a near-by table. 'Dinner is about to be served, we'll talk later.'

The meal was as deliciously rich as the surroundings in which they ate. A long table set with cobweb-fine lace mats reflected glowing silver cutlery on its polished surface. Rainbows of light prismed from fine glass and cool bowls of powder blue jacarandas deepened to exotic mauve under the light from flickering candles. When Shani hesitated before helping herself from a proffered serving dish, Tareq assured her, 'I'm sure you'll find the *Malruf* palatable—it is a mixture of minced meat and spices parcelled in vine leaves.'

Lucille found it most enjoyable, and also the baby marrows stuffed with rice, but she refused the following course, hoping her refusal would pass without comment—an abortive wish.

'Squeamish?' Tareq enquired, 'or simply replete?'

'I have eaten rather a lot.' She would have seized upon any excuse not to partake of grilled pigeons, their pathetic little corpses, split down the middle, arranged upon a bed of parsley.

He smiled, then to punish her waved away the tray of sweetmeats about to be offered as an alternative. Ruefully, she watched the tray disappear, noting that it contained fat plaits of Turkish delight stuffed with milky nuts and her favourite, *herisha*, a

94

loaf made of nuts, honey and shredded coconut. She blushed and felt foolish when Tareq caught her eye. His mischievous glint was proof that he was remembering her penchant for sweet things, so to avoid any repetition of previous teasing she turned her attention to Art, who was tucking into his meal with obvious enjoyment.

'Are the members of the crew satisfied with their new quarters, Art?'

He nodded. 'Be darned hard to please if they weren't.' He sipped appreciatively at his wine, then saluted his host with a near-empty glass. 'Thanks to Tareq and his mother each member of the crew has a comfortable room and according to the cook we brought along to provide our meals the cooking facilities are first class.' He sighed regretfully and waved away the sweet course. 'Not that we can expect meals like this one from his unimaginative hands, but perhaps it is just as well, because once filming has started there'll be very little time to spare for digesting such a repast.'

'Poor Art!' Shani cooed. 'I'll think of you slaving away in the desert while I'm enjoying the comforts of palatial living. I can't thank you enough for arranging the shooting so that Tareq and I can have a couple of weeks to ourselves before our main scenes are shot.'

'The least I could do,' he mumbled, casting an anxious look in Lucille's direction, 'considering how long it's been since Tareq's mother has had the pleasure of his company.'

Depression descended upon Lucille like a cloud at the mention of Tareq's mother. Inevitably, someone was bound to inform her of the engagement—if she had not already been informed—and the consequent confrontation would be embarrassing in the extreme. It was imperative that she accepted his proposal that she should accompany him to his study where many objects of ancient civilization were housed. 'There are some particularly fine hand-carvings which I'm sure you'll find interesting,' he smiled, pleasantly surprised by her show of enthusiasm.

'Count me out, if you don't mind,' Shani yawned unashamedly. 'Bed is the only appealing thought in my mind.'

'Mine, too ...' Art confessed, heavily overburdened with rich food and wine. 'If you don't mind, we'll say goodnight and leave you two to probe the mysterious past.'

But for once, it was not past but future events that occupied Lucille's thoughts. Tareq's study was crammed with costly and unusual items which at any other time would have captured her complete attention, but her reaction to the cases full of jade and to the exciting animal carvings—black with age and detailed with gilt except for claws of silver and eyes of alabaster—was forced—an insincerity Tareq would not tolerate. She was fingering the smooth outline of a ram without really seeing it, her mind absorbed with the problem of how to broach the subject of his mother, when he reached out to grasp her chin between his fingers. Held forcibly, she could do no other than gaze helplessly up at him.

'*Une femme douce,*' he derided gently. 'What trouble lies behind that soulful expression?'

Steadily, she confessed, 'I'm worried about deceiving your mother. She, of all people, should know the truth.'

His eyes kindled. 'Which is . . .?'

His deliberate obtuseness made her angry. 'Don't play games with me! You know that sooner or later she's bound to find out about our bogus entanglement, and the knowledge is sure to hurt—especially when I'm here under her roof, accepting her hospitality, and at the same time living a lie!'

He released her and turned to walk towards his desk. Flicking open a drawer, he picked out an object and returned to her side. He grasped her hand and she felt a circle of coldness sliding across her finger. 'There, *mon cher enfant*, the official seal of betrothal! If anyone should regard our engagement as an *entanglement*, bogus or otherwise, this ring will provide proof that such thoughts are idle speculation.'

Lucille glared at the huge yellow diamond shackling her finger. 'No!' Violently she protested as she struggled to strip the ring from her finger, but his clenched hand enclosed hers in a grip that paralysed both nerves and voice.

'Leave it!' he commanded, showing none of his earlier good humour. 'News of our betrothal has already been communicated to my mother and tomorrow, when you and she meet, she will bless both us and the ring when she officially approves my choice.'

'*Your* choice!' she choked. 'And what about me, have I no say in the matter?' When his only response was a casual shrug, she scoured his haughty features, hating the easy insolence that made him able to regard her protest as temporary pique she would soon have sense enough to discard. After all, was he not the world-renowned Tareq Hawke, idol of all women? And here, in this desert fastness, was his word not law?

'Your conceit amazes me!' she ground in her fury. 'How dare you expect me to react like a slave-girl to your commands? I won't do it! Nothing you can say will persuade me to act as a smoke-screen behind which you can conduct an affair with Shani under your mother's roof! What sort of son are you, *monsieur*? And what makes you think, knowing you as I do, that I would ever want my name linked with yours in any capacity?' Her chin tilted proudly, unafraid of lowering brows and an imperious sternness, she continued, 'You have a law which states that women have half the value of men in every sense. If that is so, then we are poor creatures, indeed, because at this moment I can think of at least one male whom I consider to be worth less respect than the dirt beneath my feet!'

'*Sacré Coeur!*' He crossed the space between them and proceeded to shake her until she fell limp against his chest. 'You are the most consistently obstinate female I am acquainted with!' he fumed, 'and your insults deserve a spanking! Luckily for you,' his hold tightened when she tried to pull away, 'I have a generous and understanding nature. Because I understand your reluctance to recognize the attraction I hold for you, I will regard your heated words as sparks generated by the heat of a heart afire!'

Speechless, she made no attempt to interrupt.

He went on to decree, 'Tomorrow I will present you to my mother as my future wife, and if you are wise you will not contradict. The situation I have manufactured suits my purpose, and although an engagement is not so binding as a marriage it will suffice for the time being. However, should you try to foil my plan by denying that any engagement exists, I will feel honour bound to prove you wrong —and, *chérie*,' he threatened softly, 'here in the desert marriages can be arranged at the snap of a finger ...'

CHAPTER NINE

LUCILLE was undecided what to wear. In fifteen minutes she was due to be presented to the Princess as her future daughter-in-law, and the prospect was daunting. All during the night she had tossed and turned, wondering if she dared tilt at the authority of the man who, since returning to his natural environment, had slipped so easily into an attitude of arrogant command doubtlessly resulting from the idolatry showered upon him since childhood.

Fretfully, she examined her reflection in a gilded mirror. She had chosen a dress of deep pink, hoping the shade might reflect colour into cheeks waxen with anxiety. Her pale cap of hair lay smoothly against a head innocently contoured, then swept into a coil of gold lying heavily against a slender neck. Her eyes were darkly grey, hauntingly lovely even though plagued by troubled thought, and as her nervous fingers clenched and unclenched bursts of yellow fire escaped the depths of the stone conferred simply to provide diamond-hard proof to Shani and any other doubters that the engagement was truly authentic.

A soft tapping on her door set her trembling. The summons she had been dreading was almost upon her and to her dismay she could not find voice to bid her visitor enter. When Tareq strode into the room she was standing stock still, too paralysed with fright to resist even when, with an oath, he cut the distance between them in two strides and enfolded her tense body into his arms. Gently he rocked her, whispering soothing words through lips that aroused deadened senses to tingling life everywhere they touched—upon eyes, cheeks, the lobe of her ear and then upon her mouth where finally they rested in a fleeting kiss of condolence.

'*Mon cher enfant,*' he softly chided, 'Maman is *une belle ange*—not the monster you suspect ...' Fear drained from her as expertly he reassured, knowing exactly the right moment to release her before embarrassment could upset the delicate balance of her emotions, then, trustful as an infant, she allowed him to lead her along passageways into the heart of the palace towards the old harem quarters. She felt blessedly alive. Anxiety was overcome by surprise; numbness by vitality, and shame by waves of sheer wanton happiness. The glow was still upon her when they entered his mother's room, a fantastic Arabian Nights interior hung with antique bronze lamps and jewel-coloured draperies. Thin, reed-like music playing softly in the background added credence to the fantasy and the dainty dark-eyed creature enthroned upon a couch piled high with silken cushions might have been Scheherazade awaiting the advent of her prince.

Keeping tight hold of her hand, Tareq presented her gravely. 'Here, Maman, is Lucille, my betrothed, fairest flower in my garden, most precious jewel in my crown.' His fingers flexed cruelly when she gasped, and his piercing look was a warning to suppress any amusement. But a very different emotion lay behind her quickly indrawn breath. Never had his voice cadences reached so tender, never had his words sounded so sincere, and most astonishing of all, she sensed in the very air between mother and son a regard so great that deceit in any form was rendered inconceivable.

For several minutes she braved dark eyes that searched her face, realizing even at that traumatic moment that the Princess was very much older than she had at first seemed. This theory was borne out when she smiled—a smile of relieved approval— and a network of tiny lines sprang into existence around eyes and mouth. 'Golden child!' her voice shook with feeling, 'fountain of warmth and light! My son need never fear loneliness once your heart is in his keeping!'

Quick tears of shame sprang to Lucille's eyes, tears which, if her life had depended upon it, she could not have suppressed. They trickled down her cheeks, great raindrops of misery culminating in a sob that escaped quivering lips. With an easy laugh, Tareq stepped into the breach by dispersing her tears with a quick swipe of a handkerchief and at the same time easing his mother's bewilderment with the words, 'This soft-hearted infant finds your approval so overwhelming, Maman, she just has to weep. Always she reacts in the same way to any great emotional experience—I dread to think what I shall do with a copiously weeping bride on our wedding day!' As he had expected, Lucille's cheeks fired, drying her tears into extinction, and his mother's expression immediately lightened.

'Then already my instinct has been proved right!' she clapped her delight. 'Guard your treasure well, my son, do not rest another day until you are made keeper of her tender heart!'

Lucille never quite knew how she survived the

following half hour of inquisition wherein the frail old lady with the will of iron probed delicately for information only to be baulked at every attempt by her equally determined son. That she was annoyed by his persistent efforts to turn the conversation away from the subject of an early wedding was made obvious when after her third unsuccessful gambit she ordered him out of the room.

'Lucille and I have matters of great importance to discuss,' she dismissed with a wave of her hand his attempted argument. 'Your refusal to treat the subject of your wedding with the seriousness it deserves is typical of your sex who know nothing and care even less about the thousand and one preparations that go into the great day.'

Even though panic-stricken, Lucille's mouth lifted faintly at the sight of Tareq's mutinous expression. The rôle of disobedient son was one she would never have imagined the virile super-star could portray, but as he reluctantly accepted dismissal resentment dragged at the corner of his mouth and the look he exchanged with his mother before he left was one of vexed indignation.

As soon as the door closed behind him the Princess began to laugh, and after an amazed second Lucille joined in. Their moment of shared insight struck them as intensely funny, and their amusement at Tareq's portrayal of injured dignity forged a bond of understanding between the old lady who still cherished the memory of him as a child and the young girl who knew him only as an authoritative man. 'I don't know how you dared!' Lucille gasped, tears of laughter streaming down her cheeks.

'Love dares anything, my child,' the Princess twinkled. 'I command my son and he obeys, but only because of the regard we share. He has always been very receptive to affection,' she mused. 'He cannot get enough, it seems, from those he loves. Yet he has never lacked attention. His father and I both adored him——' She hesitated, then seemingly questioning herself, she breathed, 'Is it possible . . .? Could a child, however cosseted and adored, feel shut out because of the great love shared by his parents . . .?'

When a tear escaped her downcast lids, Lucille quickly approached the couch and knelt to reassure. 'Mutual love and consideration are the greatest gifts parents can bestow upon their children. Only one who has known the happiness of a united family and then been deprived of it, as I was, can truly appreciate the sense of security and well-being such an atmosphere endows.'

The shadow lifted from the Princess's eyes as she looked down at the earnest, troubled face so near to her own. Her frail hand hovered above Lucille's head, then descended to stroke lightly across strands of gold. 'You have a heart big enough to encompass all the troubles of the world, *ma petite*. I think you must have been sent purposely to allay the fears that have long troubled my mind and I thank *le bon dieu* for your comforting presence and for bestowing such a blessing as yourself upon my son.'

Lucille scrambled to her feet. In her eagerness to console she had completely forgotten the deceit she was being forced to practise; far better to remain aloof than to allow the affection flowering between them to spread. 'I'd better go now before you become overtired. I'll come again soon, if I may?'

'This evening!' the old autocrat demanded. 'For too long I have pandered to this whim of Tareq's that sends him play-acting all over the world. His place is here; his people need his guidance and his strength and neither they nor I will listen to any more excuses once he has taken a wife!' She sank back against her pillows and closed her eyes, but a smile hovered around her mouth, and as Lucille tip-toed from the room she was halted by a whispered question.

'You truly love him, don't you, child?'

Without thinking, her impulsive lips formed the answer. 'Yes, Princess, I truly do . . .'

It began later that evening, a dance of the desert that continued endlessly into the night as tribesmen who gathered their news from the wind assembled at the oasis for a celebration. Enclosed within the palace, Shani fretted and fumed, taking her spite out on Lucille, whose rapt attention to all that was going on outside was reacting as tautly upon her nerves as was the non-stop beating of drums and the pounding feet of screaming dancers.

'What the blazes is going on out there?' she snapped. 'Tareq can't possibly be aware that we have been practically ordered to stay indoors because of some ridiculous custom which decrees that women must remain out of sight while the men celebrate! It really is the limit—they'll be issuing us with yashmaks next!'

'It is annoying,' Lucille agreed, tearing her eyes away from the sight of men warming drums over an open fire to tighten the skins. 'I would love to see for myself how the tribes celebrate.'

'What's it all in aid of, that's what I want to know?'

'I believe they are celebrating the forthcoming marriage of Ashra, one of the serving girls,' Lucille explained, turning away from the aperture, frustrated in her attempt to see more of the proceedings. 'Tomorrow she is to wed one of her father's tribesmen.' She frowned. 'Although when I spoke to her earlier she said nothing about the wedding being so imminent.'

'Then why are you so sure that it *is* imminent?'

'Because of the celebrations,' Lucille supplied. 'They are always carried out the night before the wedding.'

A tap upon the door seemed to represent escape from boredom, so Shani hastened to answer it. A girl glided across to Lucille, who accepted with raised eyebrows the note resting upon a silver salver. 'The Princess would like us to see some materials she thinks will make suitable dresses for the wedding,' she told an impatient Shani. 'It would be discourteous to refuse.'

'I've no intention of refusing.' Shani brightened. 'Anything is preferable to being entombed in this room for the rest of the evening.' They followed the girl to the Princess's quarters where a room was piled high with bales of cloth. Seamstresses stood around, pins and pinking shears at the ready, awaiting the moment when they made their choice. Shani's eyes glittered. She was no stranger to the fashion houses of London and Paris, but the materials on show were so fabulous as to be way beyond the means of any ordinary pocket. Immediately she pounced upon a sample of aquamarine brocade so lavishly embroidered with gold thread it would have stood up almost on its own. 'Gorgeous!' she drooled, nodding approval of the softer, paler shade of cloth indicated as a lining with which to protect the skin. Pattern books appeared as if from nowhere, and as Shani deliberated Lucille whispered awkwardly, 'Shani, do you think you should? That material looks terribly expensive, and no one has actually said that it's to be made use of by us.'

'Nevertheless, that is the idea, *ma petite*!' an amused voice spoke behind her. 'But the material I have chosen for you is not on show.' When the Princess waved an imperious hand a girl moved forward carefully carrying a slender bolt of cloth sufficient for only one dress. 'Woven from silk from my own silkworms!' the Princess beamed, waving it before Lucille's astonished eyes, 'and embroidered by the finest needlewomen in the land. Well, *ma petite*, say something! Does it please you or doesn't it?'

A nod and a croak were all Lucille could manage, but her expression of wonder was enough to bring a smile to the Princess's lips. 'Good, the child is pleased! Bring me cloth fit for a beautiful young princess, I told them, and they have done me proud, don't you think, Lucille?'

The swathe of gossamer silk was laid across her arm so that she could examine closely the fine silver threads embroidered across the face of the material. Pairs of doves were shown in loving embrace, silver leaves, crescents and stars shimmered into life at the slightest movement—conceived with love, inspired imagination and brilliant workmanship, the resulting material was too ethereal to bear description.

They spent an exciting hour poring over pattern books, discussing and rejecting, deciding and then rejecting yet again when additional designs were put forward. Shani's choice was easy, the outstandingly rich colour and texture of her material called for as simple a design as possible, whereas Lucille's delicate confection conjured up all kinds of exciting possibilities. Finally, when the Princess realized how incapable of decision Lucille had become, she offered, 'Why not leave the final choice to the seamstresses, *mon enfant*? I have the utmost confidence in their ability to decide what will best suit you, and the outcome of their choice will be a delightful surprise to both of us.'

Lucille wavered. The Princess had frowned noticeably over most of the designs, and instinct warned that the gentle suggestion was in reality more of a command. She felt she had no recourse but to agree.

'Very well, Princess Samira, if you think it best . . .'

'I do,' the old autocrat smiled her relief. 'And now that you are almost my daughter I insist you drop formality and call me Maman!'

Colour rushed to Lucille's cheeks; so determined was the Princess to accelerate the betrothal into a state more permanent that she felt she was becoming entangled in a web of gossamer-woven steel.

Unwittingly, Shani came to the rescue. 'May I also dispense with formality and address you as Maman?' she requested coyly. 'After all, my relationship with your son has progressed far beyond the stage of friendship and could advance still further should circumstances ever permit.' As her speculative glance fell upon Lucille, whose discomfort was obvious, she smiled coolly then, encouraged by her growing suspicion that Tareq was merely playing some devious game, she challenged, 'You must remember, Princess, that in our country engagements are not looked upon as binding—indeed it is becoming less and less usual in the western world for girls to marry without a first, second or even third betrothal.'

She had thought to prepare the Princess for Tareq's possible change of heart, but immediately the words were spoken she realized she had blundered. For the first time in her life she quailed as the Princess drew her body erect and flashed her a look of regal disdain.

'Are you daring to imply that my son is no longer a gentleman? Or that his regrettable absences into a community whose morals I deplore has had the effect of rendering him immune to the responsibilities of his position?' Chill hung in the air as the question hovered unanswered. 'I think not, *Miss Sharon*!' Icy emphasis was laid upon her name. 'Fame can sometimes create something out of nothing, but true nobility is inbred. It would therefore be impossible for my son to condone the frailties of an ailing society!' She swept towards the door, indignation in every line of her body, too angry with her outspoken guest to even toss a word of comfort towards Lucille whose distressed eyes followed her until she and her retinue were out of sight.

'Shani how *could* you . . . ?' She swung to face her cousin, appalled by her insensitivity and lack of tact.

'Oh, do me a favour!' Shani spat, aware that she had boobed but determined not to admit it. 'Your pandering to the play-acting of these musical comedy characters makes me sick! I came here to make a realistic movie full of blood, sweat and sex, and instead I feel I've been handed a minor role in an outdated version of The Desert Song!' Her high-pitched laughter had a decided edge—an indication that scornful though she might be, the Princess's words and manner had flicked a raw spot beneath her armour of indifference. 'I'm going to bed!' she suddenly exploded, swinging on her heel, 'and tomorrow either Tareq or Art had better supply me with some action or I swear I'll go mad!'

Slowly Lucille wandered through deserted rooms, so deep in thought that she was unaware of the shadows swallowing her slenderness into their midst, nor even of the sounds of revelry piercing the quiet indoors—madly galloping hooves, random shots from brandishing rifles, the shrieks and screams of elated tribesmen gathered around sky-licking bonfires. She was leaning with her back against a pillar, the comfort of cool marble beneath her hands somehow soothing to her fevered mind. Dusk surrounded her and her immobility was so complete that her outline could have been a slender statue moulded to the pillar of stone. She sighed, and the man approaching with cat-like tread halted, his eyes piercing the darkness. A slight movement betrayed her presence and he advanced silently until his shadow merged with hers.

'What have you been saying to Maman?' His words rasped accusingly out of the darkness.

With a gasp of fear she swung round and was

caught and roughly held prisoner. 'Tareq!' she stammered, her startled eyes attempting to seek from his expression the reason behind such restrained savagery. But the curtain of dusk held on to its secret. Then miserably she recalled his mother's distress and although she had played no part in the affair she felt partly responsible. 'I'm more sorry than I can say, Tareq, words spoken on impulse are very often regretted as I can assure you they were in this case.'

His grip tightened. 'Am I to assume then that you wish the words unsaid?'

'Of course I do!' She regarded him with amazement. 'I need hardly emphasize how angry I am with myself for allowing such a misunderstanding to occur.'

For what seemed an age he peered down at her troubled face, his stance so tense and unmoving she sensed a great inward battle taking place behind his masklike features. His fingers tightened so unbearably that she wanted to scream, but something in the air warned her to remain silent lest one more word should set spark to tinder. It was with overwhelming relief that she felt his grasp slacken, allowing some of the tension to disperse as he took a backward step into deeper shadow.

'I'm afraid,' his voice reached coolly through the gloom, 'that it is already too late to undo the damage that has been done. When my mother astounded me with the news that you were eager to become my bride a message had already been sent to the tribes and, as you will no doubt have gathered from the commotion outside, nothing less than a wedding will suffice as a climax to the celebrations.'

A rocket soared into the night sky, its passing revealing for one illuminating moment the expression of horror clamped upon her face. '*Our wedding?*' she croaked. With a sinking feeling of dread, she rushed to contradict, 'But the celebration is for Ashra's wedding, it's all been arranged, her father——'

'*Our* wedding!' he insisted gently. 'Tomorrow we go before my people as man and wife. Already the ceremony between my mother and your sponsor has taken place, but as custom decrees that your presence is unnecessary I must return alone to spend the rest of the evening with my friends while you remain inside to prepare your finery for tomorrow's presentation.'

Everything began to fall into place. The Princess's determination to have her way, the display of costly materials, the impatience of the seamstresses to begin upon the work of making the dress —*her wedding dress!* Fighting overwhelming suspicion that events might eventually overpower her, she attempted a laugh. 'It's some kind of sick joke!' she quavered. 'You're trying to frighten me, to punish me for being immune to your much publicized attraction . . .'

His answering gravity scattered her confidence to the winds. 'Here, we do not joke about such things as love and marriage.' His voice harshened. 'You may wish your words unsaid, but mere wishing will not erase them from my mother's heart.' For a second Lucille was utterly confused. She had apologized for Shani's remarks, but in any case what had they to do with her . . .

Suddenly, the reason for the dreadful misunderstanding became clear. Like an echo from the past, she heard once more the Princess's question: *'You truly love him, don't you, child?'*

And her own damning answer: *'Yes, Princess, I truly do!'*

CHAPTER TEN

SHANI was not pleased to be shaken awake by Lucille babbling dementedly about marriage, a misunderstanding, and the autocratic actions of someone insistent upon having her own way.

'Shani, wake up, I need your help! *Dear heaven,* why don't you open your eyes!' Shani struggled upright, hampered by the pressure being exerted upon her shoulders, and glared angrily.

'What on earth———!' She stopped in mid-sentence at the sight of tear-brimmed eyes and a mouth completely beyond control. 'What is it, Lucille? Has something happened to Tareq?'

Lucille slumped upon the bed as if the effort of arousing her cousin had drained her of energy. 'No, he's all right, but I'm in desperate trouble and you simply must help me. After all,' she gulped back tears, 'you are partly responsible for the whole idiotic situation.'

Shani's eyes kindled. Lucille was beyond reasoning; now might be the opportunity she had been seeking to get to the bottom of a lot she had found puzzling. Looking suitably concerned, she patted the bedcover and invited, 'Calm down, lamb, sit down and tell me everything.' The pet name she had not used since childhood brought a wavering smile of response and the years between were forgotten; it was as it used to be before Shani had developed the hard shell of self-interest so essential to the ambitious. Gratefully, Lucille began pouring out her troubles, and Shani's receptive ears missed not one nuance of a voice that softened unknowingly when mentioning Tareq's name and quivered with hurt when recounting some aspect of his deception.

Lucille felt drained but very much relieved when she had finished telling Shani everything—unaware that through hurt and panic she had betrayed a secret so deeply buried that she herself was ignorant of its existence.

'So you hate Tareq—have always hated him—and your primary wish is to put as much distance as possible between the pair of you before morning?' Shani drawled, suddenly much less approachable.

Lucille drew back. 'Yes,' she faltered, confused by a pull upon her heartstrings. 'There's no knowing what he might force me into if I don't get away. We must think of something *quickly*!'

Shani turned away to hide the glitter of eyes alive with triumph. She kept her face averted as she shrugged into a negligée, so Lucille was unaware of the effort brought to bear to conceal elation behind her exclamation of concern. 'Honestly, lamb, you're not fit to be let out alone, and Tareq ought to be ashamed of himself for taking advantage of your obvious naïveté!' A laugh escaped her, but its cruelty was covered up with the quick observation, 'But at least we'll have the satisfaction of seeing him hoist by his own petard! Just think, Tareq the wily, the confirmed bachelor, has been manoeuvred into marriage by the very person he sought to use as a shield to protect his freedom! Congratulations, my dear. Not even I could have devised a more fitting act of punishment!'

'But I've no intention of marrying him!' Lucille

protested.

'Of course you haven't,' Shani agreed, tightening her belt with a savage pull, 'but your disappearance will leave him with some very awkward explaining to do to that old despot, his mother, and I somehow think his quick wits will be taxed to the uttermost finding suitable words to smooth her ruffled feathers.'

He would find it awkward, Lucille reflected without joy. Every descendant of the House of Horus was possessed of a quick, sharp eye with which to pierce any attempted deception, and she felt a stirring of sympathy for the man whose task it would be to restore the shattered hopes of his aged mother. For one wild moment she was tempted to go through with the marriage for the Princess's sake, but sanity returned to remind her that such a course would bring unbearable heartache. To marry merely to provide a cover-up for his many affairs would be unthinkable—even though she *was* in love with him ...

Her thoughts came screeching to a halt. *What had she admitted?* Slowly, almost fearfully, she allowed the truth to seep into her mind, feeling both relief and dismay as she surrendered to the wave of love so long dammed up behind a barrier of reserve. *She loved Tareq!* She would always love him, and never more so than at this moment of blinding truth, the first and last she could ever allow herself if she were to find the courage to leave him.

'Our best plan will be to act while the celebrations are at their height.' Shani strode the length of the room, thinking furiously. 'If we manage to get to where the cars are garaged do you think you could follow the road back towards the nearest oasis?'

'I think so,' Lucille gulped. She could drive and visibility was good by moonlight, but other terrors she dared not even think about might await her in the night-shrouded desert.

'Good, then the sooner you start the better,' Shani decided, striding towards the door. 'What's wrong?' she questioned sharply when Lucille hesitated.

She swallowed hard. 'Do you think we might take Art into our confidence? He might think of a better idea—he might even offer to accompany me. I'm . . . I'm a little scared of facing the desert alone.'

With a supreme effort Shani held on to her control, but the reasonable tenor of her voice was contradicted by a foot tapping a tattoo of impatience upon the floor. 'No, I don't consider that a good idea. Men can be very clannish and he might insist upon telling Tareq. Personally,' her eyes pinpointed as she stressed, 'I'd favour a quick ride through tranquil desert before I'd suffer the indignity of marriage to a man who likens wedlock to padlock. Oh, yes, I'm aware that it was he who suggested marriage in the first place,' she overruled Lucille's protest, 'but a marriage on *his* terms, my dear, a meaningless ceremony that would barely intrude upon his life, not a solemn pact enacted before his mother and his people which they would be sure to regard as tacit acceptance of the bondage of leadership he has managed up until now to evade. You would be helping to chain a hawk, Lucille— have you the courage to withstand the battery of wildly frustrated wings?'

117

Lucille looked no match for a bird of prey as she stood with head bowed weathering fear that shuddered through her slender frame. 'You're right, of course,' she admitted huskily. 'I'd better go . . .'

They negotiated the revellers with very little trouble, hugging the shadows enclosing the brightly lit area until they reached the stables that had once housed many fleet-footed Arab stallions. One or two horse boxes were still occupied, but the majority stood empty encircling a courtyard filled with the cars and jeeps Art had hired to transport his equipment. Urged on by Shani's whispered encouragement, Lucille slipped into a jeep that had a key left conveniently in the ignition. Nervously, she turned it, depressed the accelerator, and heard the engine roar into life. The noise was deafening, so much so that Shani began waving vigorously, miming instructions to get away as quickly as possible. Casting one last desperate look in the direction of the merrymakers, she obeyed, instinctively accelerating, when out of the corner of her eye she saw figures running towards the stables with arms waving, calling out words she did not wait to decipher.

After half an hour of furious driving along the arrow-straight asphalt road she began to feel the cold. She had thrown a light coat of Shani's across her shoulders when she fled, but in her haste had forgotten the sudden drop in temperature that made extra warm covering essential once the sun withdrew its heat from the sandy dustbowl landscaped to resemble the barren surface of the moon. Her teeth were chattering and her fingers clenching the steering wheel felt permanently bunched, but up until the moment she had felt the first impact of cold fear had been the primary cause of tension, fear of the solitary unknown and of the startling animal noises that occasionally pierced the shadowy moonlight. Wolves and hyenas infested the desert, that much she knew from her research, but whether they would attack the occupant of a moving vehicle she had no way of knowing, so she gritted her teeth and drove on, praying she would soon arrive at one of the scattered rest-houses attached either to a geological mission or date-packing centre that she had often heard mentioned.

But after a further elongated period of driving her surroundings appeared just as remotely terrifying and the lonely finger of road began to appeal to her active imagination as pointing the way towards infinity. Then without warning, one of the patches of roadside shadow moved and projected itself into the path of the speeding jeep. With a scream, Lucille jerked the wheel to avoid it and was bounced and bumped unmercifully as the jeep ran off the road and raced erratically across uneven ground. For several frantic minutes she scrabbled to regain control, but the gear lever resisted the pressure of stiff fingers and the handbrake, when she eventually thought of it, proved to be useless. With a jerk that propelled her head against the windscreen the wheels stopped rotating and the bonnet nosedived into soft sand. Even though she knew the effort was abortive, desperation drove her into revving the engine hard, which resulted in the vehicle embedding itself even more firmly into sand that settled around it with the billowing softness of a feather mattress.

'*Damnation!*' Lucille jumped down, then had to

grab hold of the car door as she experienced a wave of nausea. 'Whatever shall I do now!' she muttered through a throat tight with fear. From her feet, stretching as far as the eye could see, was an ocean of rippling sand with here and there dunes rising like waves to break the monotony. The moon's face seemed to be grinning down at her as it sailed across the heavens highlighting the plight of the foolish mortal whose intelligence must be less than a grain of sand. Defiantly, she stuck out her tongue and grimaced upwards, the spirited action stirring into life a determination not to allow her celestial onlooker any further amusement at her expense. She giggled, more than a little lightheaded, then stuck out one small foot and began walking in the direction of the first of the dunes which, it seemed to her, might profitably be investigated.

She was unaware that she staggered with the gait of a drunken man across the floor of the desert. The pain of cold had completely gone, superseded by a throbbing at her temples so acute that it overruled all other discomfort. If she had remembered she might have felt grateful for the bang on the head that was responsible for the utter irresponsibility with which she travelled unfamiliar terrain, oblivious of the loneliness and uncaring of deep shadows housing sounds which earlier had sent shivers of fear along her spine. She even began to hum as she walked, unheeding of direction, into the heart of terrain dangerous even to those who were familiar with the landmarks so necessary to an ever-changing landscape.

To the Arab shepherd wrapped in a pelisse of sheepskin, she must have appeared as a ghost when she stumbled into his herd, scattering ewes and goats bleating in every direction. He cowered with fright, but then recognizing yet another forlorn waif he called snarling dogs to heel and approached, gesticulating concern, and miming his wish that she should follow him. She obeyed blindly, glad of his company, eager only for a pillow on which to rest her throbbing head.

The most cheerful sight imaginable loomed just a few hundred yards farther on. A small oasis was the site of numerous tents, bonfires cast a warming circle of light and as dogs guarding the flocks on the perimeter of the camp kept up a prolonged barking figures began spilling out of the tents, tall men, their faces bearing expressions of fierce pride, and slender, dark-eyed women who sheltered in the shadows of their menfolk as they waited for the intrusion to be explained. The shepherd urged her forward, but she shrank back, unsure of her welcome, but when the tribe caught sight of her great commotion broke out, the women laughing and gesturing delight and even the men unbending far enough to allow their expressions to assume broad grins.

'May I rest here a while?' she ventured timidly, hearing her voice as if from afar.

A bout of laughter greeted her question, but no one ventured to her assistance. She began to feel very angry. She had heard much about the courteous hospitality of the desert tribes; these people, although obviously friendly, were regarding her as if she were lost property awaiting collection by its rightful owner!

Then from out of one of the larger tents strode an

imposing figure, black-turbanned and wearing a white abbah, a flowing woollen cloak with great flourishes woven in gold thread upon the back and shoulders. The rest took a step back as he approached, leaving Lucille exposed in flickering firelight, her head bowed with tiredness, her eyes sparkling with defeated tears. She felt the ground waver beneath her feet when a voice addressed her by name.

'Was marriage to me really less preferable than any misfortune likely to befall you in the desert?' an incredibly familiar voice questioned coldly.

Her head lifted. 'Tareq?' she addressed the haughty figure, wondering if he was a figment of her imagination. In the depths of the fire a branch caught and flared, casting light across his features. She cried out in recognition and ran forward to fling herself into his arms. At the moment of impact she felt him start with surprise, but she was beyond caring whether or not she betrayed her feelings, was completely beyond resisting the wave of impetuous indiscretion that surged to a climax, then subsided into rapturous contentment when he lifted her high against his heart and carried her towards his tent with the cheers of his delighted tribe ringing in their ears.

Once inside, he set her down and stood back to examine her small pinched face with a thoroughness more than a little grim. She blinked when light cast from swaying brass lamps caught her unawares. The unexpected opulence of the interior took her by surprise and for a second her attention was completely occupied scanning rich hanging drapes, tables of hand-tooled brass, a divan piled high with silken cushions of every hue, and sheepskin rugs that curled around her frozen ankles bringing a sensation of cosy warmth. As she gazed wide-eyed with wonder, Tareq's hand lifted as if impelled to stroke away the circles, black as bruises, under her eyes, but he hesitated and slowly withdrew his fingers into a clenched fist which he then dropped to his side.

'You do not seem to have suffered unduly from an escapade that would have reduced many a brave man to despair,' he observed, his voice dangerously deep.

Lucille drew in a shaky breath, braced to withstand the anger she sensed was seething just beneath the surface. 'I'd like to explain,' she pleaded, alarmed by a riotous impulse to throw herself back into his arms and experience again the rapturous sensation of feeling his heart beating heavily in time with her own. 'I had to run away to save us both from the embarrassment of an enforced marriage. Your mother . . .' she stumbled over the lie, 'misunderstood something I said and consequently gained the impression that I was eager to become your bride.'

She dismissed as imagination an impression that he flinched from her words, and his austere answer confirmed the assumption. 'I guessed that was the case when she attempted to persuade me that you were a willing party.' When his cryptic statement drew no response, he continued grimly, 'But do you realize, I wonder, that far from escaping the fate of marriage your actions have directed you straight into the trap?'

'I don't understand . . .' she whispered, but even

123

as the bewildered cry passed her lips her conversation with Ashra was resurrected with the impact of a thunderbolt. She needed no further guidance, but as he outlined the barbaric tribal ritual her expression indicated that she had entered into a state of shock.

'The preliminaries of the marriage were performed in your absence, as has already been stated, but your presence here tonight will be a clear indication to my people that you are not merely a chosen but also a *willing* bride! You ran away. I came in search of you. At this very moment hundreds of tribesmen are combing the desert, concerned for your safety; it was mere chance that led me to stop here for a change of horse just minutes before you stumbled into the encampment.'

'Are you telling me that as far as your people are concerned we are now officially married?' she croaked, too upset to explain that the grief she displayed was being felt more on his behalf than her own. She had shackled the hawk! From now on he would be expected to shoulder indefinitely the responsibilities he abhorred. 'There *must* be a way out!' she cried, her appalled eyes searching his granite profile. 'Such a marriage isn't legal. Once we leave the oasis it can be forgotten, or else regarded as a piece of fiction—a pretence enacted to fulfil a momentary need, then discarded like an old film that has outlived its usefulness!'

A thrust of his chin destroyed her last faint hope. 'Aren't you forgetting my mother?' he countered.

Momentarily, Lucille *had* forgotten the old Princess whose hold on life seemed determined by a wish to see her son assume his rightful duties. No amount of argument would convince her that he was entitled to continue to enjoy the freedom he so greatly treasured.

He shrugged, his stern features bronzed by lamp-light into the mould of a Pharaonic mask. 'We must make the best of the situation,' he decreed with a return of his usual arrogance. 'I did, after all, intend to marry you, and although the conditions are somewhat different from those I had envisaged the obstacles are not unsurmountable.' Rancour burned in her throat. Boundless conceit had led him to believe he could have any woman he wanted; his disregard of inflicting hurt was insulting in its carelessness! She fought hard to control the dizziness that had plagued her for hours before injecting as much scorn as she could muster into the accusation. 'The conditions you had envisaged? Meaning, I take it, a cosy nest away from the madding crowd with a compliant wife to act as slave to your commands until such time as you feel an urge to escape in search of excitement?'

She could have hit him when he crooked an indolent eyebrow. 'I have had a surfeit of excitement, as you know. The picture you have just painted would suit me admirably!'

It is one thing to know yourself to be drab and unexciting, but quite another to have it confirmed. Tareq could not know that beneath the demureness of a madonna's face lay the same urge for expression felt by any wild creature yearning to be loved—and to love in return. A reckless impulse to shock overpowered her natural reticence. He was conceited, arrogant, completely selfish—but her love for him was clamouring for expression, a love which for some reason she had lost all will to conceal. Shadow-slight, she drifted towards him until she was close enough to rest her bright head against his heart. Instinctively, his arms folded around her and tightened with a convulsive jerk when she raised her head to invite his kiss. Breath rasped harsh in his throat as he acknowledged the promise of lips gently quivering and a pale flower face beautified by the intensity of an emotion he found mystifying. For once he was at a loss, but he was not a man to reason why when passion was rising. With a smoth- ered curse, he took the lips so blatantly offered and as their mouths fused he gave the lie to his state- ment of indifference to excitement by demonstrat- ing thoroughly his aptitude for revelling in any opportunity that was offered.

Lucille's ability to entice was confirmed beyond her wildest hopes. Beneath her eager caresses she felt him begin to tremble, experiencd the exhilara- tion of mastery as she returned kiss for kiss and sensed his gradual loss of control. It was a heady moment when she bit gently on his ear and heard his whispered groan for mercy, and undreamt-of delight to wield the silken whip of passion until it became bvious that his strength would not remain leashed for very much longer. She revelled in re- lease from years of repression, feeling as eager as a concubine to please her master, and when he swept her from her feet and strode with her to the divan she murmured her pleasure as his hard body pressed her deep into a nest of downy cushions.

His hand found her heart, cupped the curve of her breast: 'Rich as cream ... smooth as velvet,' he murmured thickly. *'Je t'adore, ma belle Lucille!'*

With a sigh she lowered her lashes against the on-slaught of his look, then felt a sudden sensation of swirling into space, spinning rapidly as a top out of his reach into a limbo of blackness and space un-recognizable at that moment as the oblivion of un-consciousness. From far away she heard her name called in a voice raw with vexed intent, but she was incapable of response.

She was far beyond recall when his desperate eyes spotted the bruise showing dark through a golden veil of hair. With gentle fingers he probed, then struggled slowly back to sanity as with sudden insight he assessed the bump above her forehead large and severe enough to explain the uncharacteristic, wildly uninhibited conduct that had driven them virtually to the edge of disaster. . . .

CHAPTER ELEVEN

To Lucille the following days were for ever after a confused blur. During her few clear-thinking moments she was conscious of Tareq being ever-present to soothe her with gentle words of concern and to cool her forehead with wet towels that lay like a balm upon her aching brow. Always he was there when she called, and although there were others—women who nursed her carefully through the stages of mild concussion—only his presence registered and only his voice could relax her into beneficial sleep.

On the third day she awoke clear-eyed to register her surroundings. Her brow puckered as she sought to remember where she was—and why—but though the dim interior seemed vaguely familiar the effort to remember was too much of a strain so she abandoned the attempt and closed her eyes, content to await developments. She heard a movement as someone entered the tent, but did not stir. A whiff of fresh air mingling with the aroma of a freshly smoked cigar drifted under her nose; an unmistakable clue to the identity of her visitor! Slyly she peeped, instinct warning her to act warily; for some unexplainable reason she was suffering a paralysing shyness that escalated into a burning blush when his sharp eyes caught her out. Immediately he bent closer, his expression of worry clearing as he noted the colour in her cheeks and the awareness in her now wide open eyes.

'You gave me a rough time, *mon enfant*, passing out on me like that! You are feeling better, I hope?'

She was able to nod without discomfort, but words were beyond her. His eyes held a mysterious twinkle, and he was smiling to himself as if enjoying a secret joke with which she felt sure she was in some way involved. 'What happened?' she husked finally when she could stand no more of his silent amusement. 'The last thing I remember is my arrival at this camp and your own sudden appearance, after that nothing . . .'

He placed a stool next to the divan and sat down, disconcertingly close. 'Delayed concussion,' he supplied. 'When did you get that knock on the head, have you any idea?'

Carefully she thought. 'My head collided with the windscreen when the jeep foundered,' she puzzled, 'but the blow hardly registered at the time.'

'You may not have thought so,' Tareq corrected, towering alien above clothed in the same loose-fitting outfit favoured by his Arab brothers. Then with hawk-like sharpness his expression changed. 'Perhaps it is just as well you had no idea of the dangers surrounding you in the desert! Why do you suppose shepherds keep constant guard upon their flocks?' he questioned tightly. 'And why are fires kept burning and guns at the ready?'

Her hand reached out to draw up the silken spread barely covering shoulders upon which his eyes were riveted, mirroring the tortured look of one who has seen at first hand the horrors resulting from an encounter with desert prowlers.

'Then I must feel grateful for my knock on the head,' she strove to sound flippant. 'At least the impact rendered me impervious to fear of attack by a desert savage!'

His quickly indrawn breath suggested that her words could have been better chosen and immediately she became once more aware of an atmosphere seething with implications. But after a long look his mouth relaxed into a smile that sent shivers of doubt along her spine; without the use of words it spelled out complacency, contentment to bide his time, and as he strode from the tent Lucille sank back against her pillows struggling desperately to pierce the fog behind which she felt sure lay the clue that would explain the mystery of his strange new benevolence.

They remained a further two days in the camp before Tareq pronounced himself satisfied that Lucille was fit enough to stand the journey back to the palace. On the last day she was allowed to wander amongst the tribe, making friends with the women and picking up invaluable material for the closing chapter of her book. Tareq had accompanied the tribesmen on a hunting trip into the desert and by the time they returned to camp with carcasses slung across their saddles she had long since retired and was sleeping soundly in the tent which was now regarded as her own.

Curious sounds greeted her when she awoke, the sound of beating drums, chanting, and the thudding of many feet upon bare earth. She wandered outside to look out upon a scene of festivity. Great spits were turning, scalding fat dripping from rotating carcasses was spluttering noisily into open fires and the aroma of succulent stew rose from bubbling pots to entice the appetites of men already made ravenous by a day's hunting and by the energetic dances being performed within the circle of fires. As she watched, one of the women approached carrying over her arm a swathe of patterned silk. When Lucille smiled and indicated that she might enter, the woman slipped past and laid the material on the divan before shyly making her exit.

Curiously, Lucille examined the cloth, feeling a tremor of pleasure as its softness whispered through her fingers showing a design of blue cornflowers and brilliant red poppies standing out against a background golden as sunshot sand. She shook out the folds. It was a garment crudely tailored in Western fashion but with an inevitable touch of the East in its all-concealing but form-caressing design. She had just absorbed the message that the dress had been brought especially for her to wear, when other tribeswomen arrived carrying jugs full of steaming water and a tin bath which they ceremoniously placed in the centre of the floor before tipping in the water and giggling an invitation to Lucille to take a bath. Gratefully, she thanked them before shooing them outside to stand guard while she revelled in the performance of a much appreciated ritual.

When she was ready she waited in the tent for Tareq. A quivering expectancy hung in the air, a suppressed excitement that could have resulted from the rhythmic pounding of drums and the yells of exhilarated dancers but which actually—she admitted immediately he strode through the doorway —was an outcome of his day-long absence during which time she had felt as deprived as a deserted bride. Her pulses leapt in response to his smile. Proffering an arm, he teased:

'Most favoured of women! In deference to your brave act of travelling the night desert alone the tribe have decided just this once to waive their female taboo and ask you to join them in a feast that has been prepared in your honour.'

The scarlet poppies on her dress were no brighter than the colour that rushed into her cheeks at his words, and the downsweep of confused lashes were added indication of emotions perilously unbalanced. But he seemed not to notice as he presented her to the cheering men, then escorted her towards a cushion placed upon the ground within the circle where they were about to eat.

Camel's milk, camel meat, roast mutton, bowls of stew and boiled rice were pressed upon her from all sides. Coffee—the very symbol of desert hospitality —was poured from pots resembling black and fattened geese, then platters of luscious dates, pomegranates and figs piled pyramid high were passed from hand to hand around the circle of men who as they sat cross-legged on the ground chatted, nodded and laughed while casting glances of approval in her direction. Good manners have their foundation in a respect for the feelings of others, and above all this is true of the table. Reminding herself that fingers were made before forks, Lucille tried hard not to appear squeamish when she was supplied with a hunk of bread and urged to fish out a titbit from a communal bowl of stew that had already progressed once around the circle. Blandly, Tareq ignored her unspoken plea for assistance and continued his conversation with a near companion, not quite managing to suppress a quirk of amusement.

Manfully, Lucille braved a look into the face of

the grinning Arab next to her, then daintily doubling her piece of bread into the form of a scoop, she began chasing a small piece of meat around the bowl of stew. Laughter greeted her efforts and conversation ceased while everyone enjoyed her desperate fumbling. Finally, the gravy-soaked bread collapsed into the mass and to her horror her companion's hand followed it, to emerge triumphantly holding up the piece of mutton she had found so elusive.

Her lips parted in a gasp of surprise and before she realized his intention the Arab's thrusting brown fingers had transported the titbit to her mouth. She almost choked with disgust, but before she had a chance to spit it out Tareq's fingers gripped her wrist and pressed cruelly even while, outwardly pleasant, he commanded, 'An honour has been conferred upon you. An Arab always offers the choicest morsel to his guest, but only upon the very highly esteemed is conferred the favour of having it actually placed upon his tongue! He will be most insulted if you refuse to eat.'

Lucille had no choice but to obey! Luckily, the piece of meat was small, so she drew in a deep breath and swallowed hard, hoping she would not disgrace herself by choking. Then just as she thought she was fighting a losing battle Tareq thrust a cup into her hand and she drank deeply, casting him a look of gratitude across its rim and being rewarded by a smile so tender she would willingly have suffered a repeat performance had it meant experiencing the same reward again. Then, remembering, she looked away, checking a dangerous line of thought that could lead only to unhappiness. Inasmuch as he was capable of belonging to any one person he belonged to Shani, and it would be foolish of her to forget it!

But as the long-drawn-out festivities continued Lucille was not allowed to forget that in the eyes of the tribe they were irrevocably joined together as man and wife. Frequently during the evening holy men rose to their feet calling upon Allah to bless their union with many sons—a sentiment Tareq seemed to find much satisfaction in translating—until finally emotional strain began to show itself in a pallor that glowed waxen in the moonlight and dark crescents that formed under eyes darkened almost to black with a tiredness she was struggling unsuccessfully to conceal. It was a relief when Tareq pulled her to her feet and held her strongly against his side while he begged that they be excused from further activities. His request was granted with genial nods and broad grins from the virile desert tribesmen, who understood completely a man's eagerness to be alone with his bride. They had a saying: An Arab loves in the order of: his son, his camel, and his wife—but there were times when one was allowed to take precedence over the other!

Lucille was swept off her feet into Tareq's arms and as he carried her away, leaving behind the singing tribesmen swaying in unison to the beat of hypnotic drums, a woman stepped out of the dusk to place an amulet on the threshold of the tent, calling out several unintelligible words before disappearing into the darkness.

'What did she say?' Lucille questioned drowsily as Tareq slid her to her feet inside the tent. He smiled, encircling her waist with his arm as, childlike, she snuggled against him.

'She expressed an opinion that the happiness of a woman in Paradise is beneath the soles of her husband's feet,' he enlightened humorously, seemingly not at all averse to her obvious desire to be comforted.

She looked up and was caught in the sparkle of laughing eyes. 'How strange,' she murmured, knowing quite well that she was playing a dangerous game but loath to abandon it completely. As a gesture to sanity she decided it might be wiser, since she so badly wanted to remain in his arms, to deploy him into academic discussion. 'How long will it be,' she murmured against the comfort of his hard chest, 'before the walls of the harem come tumbling down? At this very moment women still in purdah are studying hard, dark eyes behind masks still serene, but dark minds stretching and growing ...'

He treated the question seriously, sombrely observing, 'It is true that in the few remaining harems learning is very much in the air—and learning leads to change. Older ones, such as my mother, will not accept that change is inevitable, and so they remove their minds from what must happen and pretend the fact does not exist.'

Drowsily content, she questioned, 'Are you resentful of your mother's refusal to live in what must be to her an unacceptable present?'

She felt his shrug, then thrilled to the touch of his cheek against her hair. 'Resentful is too strong a word—impatient, perhaps, as are so many of my contemporaries, men with ideas modern enough to relish the trappings of a civilized society but who, for the sake of aged parents, relinquish from time to time the comfort of a limousine and an executive's desk for the dubious delights of a camel and a tent.' His tone betrayed the futility of trying to impose new standards upon minds attuned to the customs of centuries past, and Lucille felt sudden shame at the knowledge of how little justice she had meted out to the man whose unconcerned attitude to life had so successfully hidden deep concern for others. It was an incredible thought—one Shani would laugh to scorn—that Tareq the Hawk should have hidden beneath his armour of indifference an emotion as unselfish as concern!

She lifted her head, eager to convey remorse, but he had had enough of talk; the surrounding solitude, her nearness and her obvious lack of distaste for his company were not conducive to the success of serious discussion. He lowered his head and swooped upon her upraised mouth with the precision of a bird of prey to carry off both mind and body to previously unreached heights. At first she was a willing captive, content to be borne along at a speed breathtakingly swift, too embroiled in the delights of her newly discovered love to remember the darker side of his nature—the side that decreed that, like a spaniel, the more one beats a woman the more she'll fawn ...

It was only when his hand cupped her breast that she recalled from the dim recesses of her mind a similar earth-shattering sensation. She pulled away, alarmed and doubtful. The reactions aroused by his touch had answered a hitherto unrecognisable yearning of nerves and impulses once driven to a peak of expectancy and since left quivering, urgently desirous of revival. His inscrutable smile, his expression of inner satisfaction, the impression she had formed that for some reason he was content to bide his time, were all in some way connected with a vague dream that for days had tortured her subconscious—a dream wherein unbridled emotions had reached a passionate climax only to subside with sudden cruelty and plunge her into a pit of deprived darkness.

'Tareq!' she resisted when he reached out to draw her back into his arms. 'I must know ... I half remember ...' On the verge of tears she appealed, 'Did something happen between us that first night? Did I do anything that would place me in the same category as those women whom you pretend to despise but whose companionship you nevertheless seem to find ... satisfying?'

He hesitated, harrowed by the frustration of a man twice deprived, then mustered sufficient control to answer casually, 'I have always found your company satisfying, *chérie*, even when you have been deliberately obstructive, as you are being now. Why, I wonder, do you find it necessary to intrude pointless discussion into every moment of intimacy? Is it your form of defence against siege, do you perhaps use rhetoric as a lifeline, employing a string of words to haul yourself out of difficulties whenever you find yourself in danger of being swept away on a current of strong emotion?'

Humiliation flamed her cheeks. He might just as well have accused her outright of being a cheat as imply that she was the sort of girl who delighted in arousing in a man emotions she had no intention of satisfying. All the doubts she had ever felt returned to haunt her. He was an expert philanderer, so satiated by the attentions of the world's most beautiful women he found a perverse delight in breaking down the resistance of the only woman who had not shown willingness to fall into his arms. Insipid, timid and unworldly she might be, but to him she represented one single failure in a lifetime of amorous successes!

Slim and defiant in the gown of many colours donned especially to give him pleasure, she charged, 'Do not condemn me for an inbred aversion to behaviour I consider degrading, *monsieur*. I do not consider myself a prude, but I refuse to sacrifice to the form of hypocrisy which entails my having to provide myself with an excuse for any of my actions!'

Fire flickered behind storm-flecked eyes as he weathered the onslaught. The very air around them seemed alive with animosity—his anger—her contempt. She faced him bravely, vulnerable in the way a woman is always vulnerable to a man's superior strength, but anger had given her courage so she felt no fear when he strode forward with fists clenched to deliver a verbal blow almost physical in its savagery.

'If the question you want answered is: did we make love? then the answer is yes!' When she flinched he tormented her further, seeming to derive great satisfaction from purging his aggravation by inflicting intolerable pain. 'But I see no reason to make a tragedy out of an action carried out merely to ensure that you never again attempt to run away. We were then—as we are now—man and wife, so for heaven's sake stop looking at me as if you consider me the devil incarnate and let us reason out the situation sensibly!'

Sensibly! Never in her life had Lucille felt such bitter loathing for a fellow creature! With a few sadistic words he had ripped apart the whole fabric of her life, reduced her to the level of a concubine and filled her with such shame she felt she could never face society again. On a deep shuddering breath she damned him, 'I hate and despise you! How . . .' she choked on scalding tears, 'how can you possibly seek to justify such an action by employing the excuse of a marriage you know will not stand up in a court of law either in your country or my own?'

A muscle twitched in his cheek, but his eyes did not waver. 'Hate and scorn never came in tears,' he derided, his coolness driving her demented. 'There is little sense in making yourself ill over a happening which, if you are honest, you must admit was inevitable, if perhaps a little premature.'

Against such adamant conceit, argument was impossible. And besides, Lucille was feeling so deathly tired there was not an atom of fight left in her. With a gesture of defeat she threw herself down upon the divan and hid her face amongst the pile of cushions, soft enough to muffle her sobs and to absorb a multitude of heartbroken tears. Whipped by his tongue, lashed by his contempt, she was left alone to lick her wounds. The lamb had dared to challenge the hawk—and, predictably, the hawk had drawn blood!

CHAPTER TWELVE

THEY set out for the Oasis of Behdat the following morning in the jeep tribesmen had salvaged from its bed of sand. The journey which, when Lucille had travelled it alone had seemed to take a thousand years, was accomplished in a matter of hours that seemed less even though silence was their constant companion.

Her brain was aching with thought; a night of ceaseless tears had left her drained of anger and the hatred she had charged Tareq with during their violent scene had abated to a dull hurt that throbbed incessantly through heart and body. He had questioned once: 'Can I rely upon your co-operation once we reach the palace?' and though she had not replied with words her derisory laughter that had ended on a half sob had seemed to supply the answer he sought. *What was she to do?* For some insane reason she felt bound to him—as irrevocably bound as the tribe would have her believe. Not because of marriage rites that had been performed without her knowledge or consent, but because of the physical union for which, honestly forced her to admit, she was probably as much to blame as he. She shifted in her seat, embarrassed by vague memories, and his eyes swivelled from the road querying her discomfort. Immediately she coloured and turned away; his glance could reach her soul and he must never be allowed to sense the reaction his concern culled from her sorely tried emotions.

Lucille was aching with weariness by the time Tareq swung the jeep into the palace courtyard. Servants came running from every direction, calling praise upon Allah for her safe deliverance. Gratefully she allowed Ashra to lead her to her room, to run her bath, then to tuck her between cool sheets in a dimmed, air-conditioned bedroom. Via the desert grapevine news had reached the palace of her illness, so Ashra had no need of Tareq's sharp reminder to treat his wife with care and to bestow upon her every possible attention.

Hours later Shani entered her bedroom just as she was opening her eyes. The room which earlier had owed its dimness to shutters closed against the sun was now full of evening shadow, and as Lucille struggled to sit upright Ashra entered to light lamps that swung under her touch, throwing Shani's elongated shadow upon the walls. Lucille shrank from the anger on her cousin's face.

'You sly cat!' Shani berated without preliminary. 'I believe you deliberately allowed him to catch you up!'

Lucille bit hard to steady a trembling lip. The long sleep which ought to have refreshed had instead left her feeling weaker than before and far from relishing a verbal battle she would have agreed to anything rather than embark upon an argument. She sighed wearily and whispered agreement. 'You could be right . . .'

A hissed breath, cutting as a sword, was Shani's initial reaction, then she swung a vicious look upon Lucille's white face and directed, 'So! At last we're getting near to the truth! Far from hating Tareq you've deliberately thrown yourself in his path on every conceivable occasion and, devious brat that you are, have eventually managed to manoeuvre him into a situation compromising enough to force his hand! But mark this, my innocent—Tareq and I were meant for each other, and it will take a cleverer woman than yourself to keep us apart!' She gave a coarse laugh and withdrew a few steps from the bed with the hurtful observation. 'Look at you! Sugar and spice and all things nice ... ! Can you honestly believe yourself capable of holding the interest of a man idolized by millions? Tareq's world is the world of action, suspense and excitement, so roll up your carpet of dreams, my dear. Cottages and carpet slippers are simply not his scene!'

Tareq's behaviour at dinner that evening seemed to bear out everything Shani had said. He was restless, brittle in conversation and moodily bent upon finding disfavour with everything offered. His meal went almost untouched as he waved away each carefully prepared course with an impatient hand, then he underlined his boredom by insisting upon rolling up rugs so that Shani and he could dance to music blasting discordantly from a portable record player. Lucille's instinctive reaction was to turn to Art for comfort, completely unaware, as they became engrossed in conversation, that Tareq's attention was upon their closely held heads. Art wanted to be told everything about her experience in the desert, so willingly she launched upon the tale, recounting the pleasanter aspects of her stay with a smile upon her lips and a sparkle in eyes previously sad.

Unfortunately Art, who found her account of the day-to-day happenings within a nomadic tribe intensely interesting, became so carried away that he forgot the need for caution and in a loud voice congratulated her warmly. 'Unbelievable!' He eyed her with renewed respect. 'What fantastic material! If the rest of your book is as interesting as the last chapter promises to be then it's bound to make for compelling reading. Congratulations, sweetheart, success is a cast-iron certainty!'

His words coincided with a break between records and echoed through the room with the clarity of a proclamation. Shani swung round, her face a picture of curiosity, but Lucille had eyes only for Tareq, whose impassive features gave away less than did his tone when he drawled, 'Interesting! May we be allowed to share more of the obviously long-standing secret?'

Lucille grew hot and cold under his scrutiny. Love, even if unreturned, bestows insight, and she was half puzzled, half afraid of the resentful undertones threaded through the supposedly negligent enquiry. Jealousy was too ridiculous a supposition to apply to Tareq, but there was no doubting his annoyance at having to apply to Art for answers.

Art's apologetic expression cleared when with reluctance she nodded permission to speak, realizing that even the little that had been said had made it impossible to insist upon continued secrecy. Relishing the opportunity of scoring against Shani, Art obliged.

'This talented child has not only written a book, she also has a definite promise of publication once the final chapter has been completed!' Lucille's triumph might have been his own as he revelled in the silent astonishment his words created. Shani was obviously dumbfounded, while Tareq's expression-less face could have been carved from stone.

Exploiting his role of privileged confidant to the limit, Art waxed enthusiastic. 'Aware as we all are of Lucille's dislike of limelight, you'll understand her reluctance to spread the news—indeed, she only confessed to me under pressure because at the beginning there was some doubt about her ever reaching Egypt and she was at her wits' end to find some way of achieving her object. Each chapter of her book deals with the customs of a different race, you see,' he enlightened them kindly, 'and it was imperative that she reach Egypt in order to research the final chapter.' He slanted a sly grin towards Shani, enjoying her jealous discomfiture and the chagrin which not even her acting capabilities could conceal.

Goaded by his satisfaction, she turned upon Lucille. 'And you dared to use me to further your own ends! All these months while you've been fed, clothed and transported everywhere at my expense you've neglected your duties to go haring off to collect material for this book! You cheat!' she exploded, her rage escalating, 'I'll expect you to refund every penny of the money it's cost me to finance your travels!'

'*Cost you!*' Art hooted, allowing his indignation free rein. 'Come off it, Shani. Lucille's slaved for every penny she's earned! Personally, I'm astonished she found it possible to cram any research at all into the very few spare hours you allowed her.'

Tareq interrupted with the cold observation, 'Nothing will be achieved by abortive accusations. Indeed, if we examine our motives carefully it will become evident that the same charge can be levelled against each of us!' The bleakness of his look froze Lucille's heart; though deeply involved, he seemed to have set himself aloof from the tableau, his judgement sounded that of an uninterested onlooker! She writhed inwardly, wondering at the implication behind his words, then was shocked when he continued to clinically analyse. 'You, Shani,' he directed gravely, 'must admit to a selfish misuse of Lucille's services—she owes you nothing! I too am guilty. Concern for my own interests was the motive behind our engagement. Very much against her will—or so I believed at the time—I persuaded her to masquerade as my fiancée, then embarrassed her by involving her in marriage plans too complicated to be immediately resolved.' Lucille felt the full force of his displeasure when he looked directly into her pinched, colourless face. 'Please accept my apologies for the inconvenience you have suffered. Unfortunately, for my mother's sake, I must ask you to bear with the situation for just a few days longer. You will then become entirely relieved of obligation.'

'Obligation . . .?' she queried with startled inflection.

He nodded, then smiled thinly. 'But yes,' he confirmed. 'My mother loves you dearly—does not such love place upon the loved one an obligation to respond—with pity, if not with affection?'

He held her look, daring her to deny responsibility towards the well-being of the old princess who yearned to set a seal of blessing upon their marriage. Lucille's lacerated feelings rebelled at the idea of suffering yet again, but there was no doubt what it was Tareq expected—an assurance that she would play out the charade to the bitter end. Her eyes darkened as unconsciously she pleaded for release from further emotional pressure, but when his forceful adamancy did not waver her head bowed and she sighed. As he said, a couple of days would soon pass, and compared with the traumatic experience of being married by proxy the final act of blessing could be borne with fortitude.

'Very well ...' he barely heard her whispered capitulation, 'two more days.'

'Thank you.' He squared his shoulders as if he, and not she, had accepted a burden, then chilled her heart with words of icy displeasure. 'In return, may I say how gratified I feel to have been of use? Your initial reluctance to fall in with my plans had me completely fooled—a less competent actress would have betrayed some signs of eagerness. However, the fact that you used the engagement to further your own ambitions has relieved me of the ridiculous self-reproach that has plagued me for days. Once my mother has been pacified arrangements can be made to continue filming elsewhere so that we can leave the oasis together, then go our separate ways without her becoming aware of the deception.'

Lucille's stomach revolted as he outlined the cruel plan. Deceit seemed to come as naturally to him as breathing, but, as he had earlier reminded her, were they not all equally guilty? Self-disgust washed over her; she felt soiled, degraded at the idea of playing a part in the fooling of his unsuspecting mother. She spun on her heel and ran towards the door, not daring to delay even long enough to reply to Art's anxious enquiry lest her voice should quiver with an overspill of blinding, unreasonable tears.

She had been in her room less than half an hour

when the Princess honoured her with a visit. It was a great concession; as a rule she never left her own quarters but summoned others into her presence. The enormity of the favour being bestowed was evident from Ashra's expression of awe as she bowed the Princess across the threshold.

'*Ma petite!*' the Princess greeted Lucille as she hastened forward. 'How proud you have made me, and how very, very happy!' She accepted a proffered chair, then chattered on, seemingly oblivious of Lucille's bewilderment. 'I had not expected you to treat our customs with such a degree of enthusiasm—Tareq does not, even though I scold him often for the omission—but you, *chérie*, acted very bravely. Were you not terrified alone in the desert? Even though you must have guessed Tareq was not far behind, the desert at night can be *très terrible*! And your poor head! Forgive me, child, for not enquiring sooner—are you still suffering discomfort from the injury?'

Her concern was comforting and Lucille's young heart opened to it like a bud to the first warmth of spring. 'I am perfectly well, Maman,' she made use of the treasured name, 'a little tired, perhaps, but that can easily be remedied.'

'Hmm . . .' As the keen old eyes wandered thoughtfully over her face Lucille widened her smile, unaware that its forced brightness was contrasting sadly against swollen eyelids and cheeks painfully salted with the passage of tears.

Delicately ignoring all signs of anguish, the Princess probed, 'Tareq is in the main salon dancing with your cousin, I believe?'

She had not asked why, but Lucille sensed she

was obliquely questioning her presence alone in her room, and consequently she felt compelled to make excuses. 'Yes, they are. Art and I joined them there after dinner, but I ... I suddenly felt very tired.' With head bowed she slid to her knees at the Princess's feet, ashamed to fabricate further, and a short second later felt a gentle hand upon her head.

'This girl, Shani ... she is in love with my son?'

Lucille stirred but did not look up. 'In love? ... I'm not sure. She finds him very attractive,' she admitted in a gulp.

The hand continued to stroke. 'A clever distinction, *mon enfant*, the gold and the dross, eh? How happy I am in my belief that Tareq, too, is clever enough to recognize the distinction.'

Lucille stiffened, suddenly aware that the Princess was possessed of an astuteness of vision that made nonsense of their attempted deception. She knew perfectly well that Shani held a vital place in Tareq's affections and her well-laid plans had been designed to combat an alliance she feared might escalate into an unacceptable marriage. A dull pain made itself felt in the region of her heart as once again she felt conscious of being used. The affection she felt for the Princess had been a spontaneous thing, born of happy accord, but the reciprocal affection she had imagined did not exist; what she had thought of as love had turned out to be merely an old woman's approval of her worth as a dutiful wife for her son ...

Carefully, she withdrew from the Princess's reach and walked with as much dignity as she could muster towards the window. Drifting upward was the sound of music and Shani's contented laughter as, twirled in Tareq's arms, she danced past the window of the salon far below. Suddenly nothing seemed to matter any more—not Shani, not the Princess, not even Tareq. She wanted to go home, yearned to leave the Palace of Horus and its predatory occupants far behind. When the Princess's voice penetrated through her misery she swung round, ready to promise anything that might accelerate her departure.

'My people are anxiously awaiting the public blessing. When do you think you will be well enough to go before them as Tareq's bride?'

'Tomorrow!' Lucille rasped, ruthlessly stamping down upon stirring conscience. She could no longer be fooled; the Princess, in the manner of the aged, was determined to have her way and gratification alone was responsible for the look of fond regard she was projecting from eyes laden with joyful tears ...

In a flutter of excited anticipation she returned to her quarters, leaving Lucille pacing her bedroom plagued with indecision. In just two more days she would be free. A whole exciting new life beckoned, a life independent of Shani's domination, full of work so satisfying it promised to be more of a pleasure than a chore. Why then did she feel so miserable? Everything she had hoped to achieve was within reach; in forty-eight hours she would be leaving behind for ever the Palace of the Hawk and its cruel master!

Her restless prowling ceased as she reached a decision. All she needed was final reassurance—confirmation from Tareq's own lips that nothing would be allowed to delay her departure once the ceremony of public blessing had been accomplished. Without further thought she ran out of her room, music still drifted in the air, which seemed to signify Tareq's presence in the room below—she would not sleep until his definite promise had been extracted!

At the head of the stairs she slowed pace. Lamps which might have guided her steps had not yet been lit, so carefully she negotiated the steps, her soft-slippered feet treading silently across great slabs of marble. The sound of music grew louder as she approached the salon, but there was no laughter and the absence of voices accentuated her feeling of solitude.

She appeared like a wraith in the doorway, a slender, forlorn figure too indeterminate to impinge upon the minds of the couple standing closely entwined in the centre of the room. Lucille's sharp gasp seemed to reverberate around the shadows, but Tareq and Shani were too utterly absorbed to notice. She knew she should have retreated, but her feet felt frozen to the floor, awaiting guidance from a shocked, immobile mind.

'Darling,' she heard Shani whisper, 'when are you going to admit your true feelings—how much longer must I fight your reluctance to admit surrender?'

Lucille winced when Tareq tilted Shani's chin and dropped a light kiss upon her pouting mouth. 'Be patient, *ma petite*, for just a few days longer ...'

Lucille's vision was restricted to a view of his broad shoulders and proud head, but Shani must have found his expression encouraging because her arms slid around his neck as she pressed closer against him. 'We'll make a devastating partnership, my sweet!' she cooed. 'Between us, we'll conquer the world, producers will vie for our services and I foresee that eventually there'll be no limit to the percentages we can demand from our films!'

Tareq sounded amused. 'Obviously you have given a lot of thought to our future,' he teased, then a little more sombrely, 'Have you also decided what is to become of Lucille once we leave the oasis?'

Shani sounded as shocked as Lucille felt upon hearing her own name mentioned. 'Lucille?' The softness of her tone gave way to sharpness. 'She'll go her own way, of course. She's already caused us far too much embarrassment and I really couldn't stand much more of her mooning around! You do realize, my darling,' she questioned silkily, 'that the little fool is hopelessly in love with you?'

'Really?' That one bored word threatened to tear the heart from Lucille's breast. So disinterested was he, his attention was riveted upon a mirror directly in front of him. The eternal actor! She struggled to whip up scorn even through waves of pain. How could she have been misguided enough to fall in love with a man so shallow that even his real-life actions were carefully studied, performed as if before whirring cameras? She willed herself to flee, but seemed fated to remain until her humiliation was complete.

'Certainly!' Shani trilled, triumphant. 'But if you feel any chivalrous impulse to make amends you can forget! I've no doubt that during your sojourn in the desert you proved your reputation up to the hilt, and I consider that the experience is reward enough for a meek little madam who'll no doubt cherish the memory for the remainder of her uneventful life!'

A question lay behind the jealously-flung statement and Lucille felt every drop of blood drain from her face as she waited, expectant any second of hearing Tareq begin an amusing résumé of the degrading interlude. But his response was muffled, sounding more like a muttered imprecation, and she remained swaying in the doorway just long enough to see him pull Shani into his arms to silence her with an intense, prolonged kiss.

CHAPTER THIRTEEN

In her dress of white silk embroidered with silver crescents, stars and other symbols of superstition designed to ward off the evil eye, Lucille looked youthfully virginal. Ashra fussed around her, trying to contain stray golden hairs within a coiffure skilfully arranged to show off jewelled hair ornaments bestowed by the delighted Princess upon her new daughter. A further bounty was a broad anklet of beaten gold, intricately engraved, which fettered Lucille's slender ankle like a slave-girl shackle. 'A very precious heirloom,' Ashra had assured her. 'Many tourists haunt the bazaars of Cairo seeking such anklets, but as each family guards its heirlooms jealously there are very few to be found.'

Lucille tried to infuse interest into her reply, but Ashra was not deceived. Her eyes radiated doubt, and puzzlement as to why the most favoured of brides, one who had found favour with the mighty desert hawk, should be reflecting such lack of joy. Lucille sighed. In a few moments Tareq would be arriving to escort her outside where hundreds of tribesmen and their families had gathered to demonstrate their respect and to approve his choice. Reluctantly, she pushed her toes into slippers of soft white kid, then stood up to survey the results of Ashra's labours reflected in a full-length mirror. From head to toe she sparkled, diamonds at her throat and wrists, emeralds in her ears, and in the centre of her forehead—suspended from a fine gold chain—another larger emerald flashing green fire. Outwardly she looked radiant; inwardly she felt dead, as coldly worthless as a pile of burnt-out ashes. With a wave of her hand she dismissed Ashra, who was advancing towards her carrying a wisp of gauze.

'No yashmak!' she declared firmly, showing the first spark of animation Ashra had seen from her that day.

'But, my lady, it is customary! No bride can be considered respectable without ...' A rap upon the door interrupted the argument and she flew to open it, expectant of an ally. Lucille waited while Tareq was admitted, feeling less emotion than she would had some strange desert nomad strode into their midst. He brought with him a breath of desert air, looking magnificently virile in dazzling white shirt and breeches beneath an *abbah* flowing blood-red from his shoulders. Knee-boots of polished leather gleamed beneath the cloak as he advanced into the room, filling it with a presence she ought to have found intimidating but which, in this instance, barely merited a shrug. With eyes kindling, he relished her beauty, then his glance sharpened as he sensed her detachment. Ashra seized the silent moment to air her grievance, and as he listened a frown began to form which, when he eventually dismissed her, had deepened into a scowl. When his lips parted to speak Lucille forestalled him.

'I will not wear a yashmak, and that is final!' Her voice trembled on the words, but as he scoured her pale features no emotion other than defiance was allowed expression. She braced herself for argument. In the past Tareq had overruled her every objection, but on this count she was determined to succeed in her vow not to wear the flimsy symbol of woman's absolute subjugation to man's will.

His sudden smile took her by surprise; it projected understanding and a hint of benevolence. However, he paid her the compliment of complete gravity when he assured her softly, 'Behind the veil our women are cosseted and cherished to an extent unknown in Western society. Do not despite them too much, *chérie*, for clinging to a custom which they know in their hearts is most beneficial to themselves. What man would not feel gratified by the knowledge that in all of God's garden one flower blooms for his eyes alone? And does it not follow that when man is flattered his instinctive urge is to reward well the one who has fulfilled his need?'

'Flattery, *monsieur*, is like perfume, which wise men may sniff but only fools will swallow!' Lucille scoffed, suppressing a tremor of weakness.

'Are you daring to imply that I am a fool?' In one stride he swallowed the distance between them. Not for the first time he was unendurably near, radiating a power that left her quivering, but this time there was a difference, his pride was flicked on the raw, the pride of Pharaohs who for centuries had been the subject of adoration and praise.

She had not imagined him so vulnerable! The ragged edge of his voice contained the violence of wildly beating wings. 'Perhaps,' his teeth were set on edge, 'it amuses you to see how easily fools are vexed? I had thought you different, but like all women you seem to find sadistic pleasure in giving a twist to the screw!'

She backed away, confused. 'Forgive me, *mon-*

sieur, I had no wish to offend, I spoke in haste . . .'

—On a high tide of anger he quoted savagely: 'The world is full of fools, and he who will not admit it should live alone and smash his mirror, isn't that what you think, *ma belle tormenteuse*?'

'Not . . . not exactly,' she stammered, not trusting the meteoric rise and fall of his passion. 'I was merely pretending to be clever, actually the sentiment expressed was not even original, just a remark stored up in my memory for just such an occasion.'

His proud head tilted and for what seemed an age Lucille trembled under the lance of his displeasure. Then to her amazement he broke into soft laughter. 'You have no need to pretend cleverness, little lamb,' he assured her, controlling twitching lips with difficulty, 'your ability to disarm is a quality rarer than mere intelligence and far more effective!'

Tentatively she returned his smile, puzzled, but too relieved to question his rapid change of heart. Instinct told her that for a moment she had been in real danger, and in that same moment she had glimpsed a violence so terrible she knew that never again would she find the courage to tilt at his authority or to walk other than on tip-toe over his astonishingly sensitive feelings. He extended an arm and when she placed her hand in the crook of his elbow he dryly remarked, 'You may dispense with the yashmak if the wearing of it offends you, but if your face is to remain uncovered I must insist upon a change of expression. No man relishes pity, and I refuse to appear before my friends accompanied by a bride who looks as if she is about to enter the gates of hell!'

The Princess and her retinue were arranged, magnificently dressed, around a large balcony overlooking the courtyard. Below, every available space was crammed with people and every street and alleyway leading to the palace held hundreds more jostling for vantage points from which to follow the proceedings. Tareq led his bride towards two silken cushions positioned at the foot of the Princess's chair, and as they knelt, awaiting her blessing, Lucille was very aware of Shani, breathtakingly lovely in her brocade grown, watching with a cynical smile predominant upon her lips.

The ceremony was moving in its simplicity. The Princess, whose dignity could never be questioned, had assumed an added regality and only iron will prevented her from marring the solemnity of the occasion with proud tears. Her hands trembled, however, when she placed one on each of their heads and she had to struggle to keep her voice firm as she intoned the traditional words of blessing. Complete silence fell over the crowd as they followed her every word, the only sound coming from film technicians and camera crews who, though more than a little sceptical, were nevertheless determined to record the event on film.

It must be similar to playing a part in a movie, Lucille thought as she obeyed Tareq's whispered instruction to stand. In a dream, she moved with him towards the edge of the balcony to look down upon a sea of faces, then, as the Princess took hold of her hand and placed it within Tareq's, a great roar of approval greeted the action, a roar that continued to gain in volume until the ancient palace foundations were threatened.

'Good girl!' Tareq whispered against her ear, his

smile tightening an extra squeeze upon a heart already constricted. Out of the corner of her eye Lucille saw Shani advancing towards them, her fixed smile at war with the jealous glint in her eyes. Tareq must not have noticed her; he began ushering Lucille in the wake of his mother who, after one last wave to the cheering crowd, was making her way indoors to where a banquet had been set out for the benefit of visiting sheiks. From then on Shani's approach was cut off. For almost two hours Lucille stood at Tareq's side being presented to dignitaries who examined with varying degrees of approval the pale, slender girl, searching her great eyes—grey as wood smoke—before turning away seemingly satisfied with what they saw.

They were sipping champagne, admiring a pile of presents pyramid-high, when Shani eventually caught up with them. Tareq was indicating the finer points of a silver-embossed bridle and Lucille, her shyness giving way to admiration, was stroking the supple leather and attending carefully to his instructions.

Shani could understand the necessity of performing before an audience, but the discovery that their absorption in each other was genuine she found utterly galling. 'Thank goodness we'll be leaving all this behind us soon!' she interrupted, visibly aggravated, then, linking her arm within Tareq's, she appealed, 'Please, darling, take me out of here. I'm sure you must be as sick as I am of this meaningless charade.'

Lucille coloured furiously. Just for a moment she had been as absorbed as any new bride with the concrete expressions of goodwill bestowed by their guests—even to the extent of wondering where in the palace might be displayed to the best advantage the priceless vases, bolts of silken cloth and colourful, intricately patterned rugs. Tareq, too, seemed to consider the interruption untimely and for a second before removing Shani's arm from his sleeve his eyes flashed a warning. Then suavely he reminded her, 'Today must be lived if tomorrow is ever to dawn. Contain your impatience until our visitors have left; men of the desert are becoming slowly acclimatized to change, but they are far from ready to accept the sight of a bridegroom with two women hanging upon his arm.'

He was right. Lucille could feel the questioning looks being levelled from all sides and hear voices raised in surprise at Shani's unforgivable lack of propriety. Then the Princess's voice reached out above the babble, calling out instructions Lucille could not interpret in a tone that rang with encouragement. It was puzzling the way in which the younger men reacted. With a delighted roar they surged forward, encircling Tareq and herself, then urged on by shouts of encouragement they began tightening their ranks, slowly advancing until she and Tareq were trapped within an increasingly diminishing circle.

'*Damnation!*' she heard Tareq expel under his breath, then he barely had time to mutter: 'I'm sorry about this, I ought to have remembered——' before the horde descended and she was lifted from her feet and borne away on a wave of supporting arms. She did not struggle because she felt no fear. Tareq was suffering the same treatment, and though he must be fully aware of the outcome of the exercise he was smiling, so obviously there was nothing to fear. Though her captives were boisterous, the hands that held her were gentle, careful not to bruise.

At breathtaking speed, they ascended the stairs, then set off in triumph down a corridor, stopping outside of an unfamiliar door and easing Lucille to her feet as they reached the threshold. Tareq's smile was good-humoured but helpless. Overwhelmed as he was by a crowd of determined youths he could do no more than shrug in answer to her bewildered look. Then once again she was lifted, this time by Tareq, who caught her in his arms and carried her over the threshold into a room sumptuous in appointment, its one main object of furniture a large, accommodating bed. Lucille stiffened, shocked by all kinds of alarming possibilities, then fell breathless as he dropped her amongst the pillows before striding to kick shut the door upon a bevy of grinning faces.

She struggled upright when he retraced his steps to stand brooding down at her. She suspected he was searching for the least offensive words with which to explain away the embarrassing situation, but Ashra had already outlined the ceremony enacted by friends of the bridegroom to ensure privacy for the 'deflowering of the bride'. She had laughed to scorn the idea of being made to participate in such a custom, treating the whole thing as a joke too unbelievable even to discuss, yet here she was, imprisoned with hm in an atmosphere of seduction created especially to aid an eager bridegroom relax his apprehensive bride!

Her cheeks felt afire as she swung from the bed

and stood up to challenge him. 'Consider the obligation I owed your mother discharged as from this moment, *monsieur*. Nothing you can say or do will persuade me to become involved in any further activities pertaining to this mock marriage!'

Thick, dark lashes lowered, but momentarily she glimpsed a spark, tinder-bright, that flashed, then subsided into a smouldering so fierce she quivered with apprehension. With a violence that hurt Tareq swung away, snapping the chain anchoring the cloak around his shoulders with a vicious tug so that it fell like a pool of blood on to the pastel-shaded carpet. Her eyes followed, riveted by an action synonymous with the throwing down of a gauntlet— and as terrifying! She backed away when he began to laugh, soft, meaningful laughter that froze to immobility clamouring senses screaming a warning to run from the man whose veneer of ultra-sophistication had been stripped with the speed of a discarded cloak to reveal a primitive—an arrogant, possessive sheik of the desert!

With the swiftness of a hawk he strode towards her, pouncing upon slim shoulders with talons of steel, drawing her forward until her forehead was level with lips that coaxed even as they demanded.

'Don't be afraid, *ma gentille épouse*, relax here in my arms where your shy young heart will begin to stir, then eventually to yearn for the exciting onslaught of fierce, all-consuming passion.'

A wave of crazy weakness set her swaying against him and as his arms tightened his soft growl of satisfaction, no louder than a whisper, sounded a trumpet of derision in her ears.

What a weak fool she was!

She tore out of his arms, hating both him and herself for the storm of feeling that almost weakened her resolve to put as much distance as possible between herself and the exciting devil whose whole life was dedicated to the pursuit of pleasure. Small beads of perspiration stood out on her forehead as she backed far enough away to deride with safety, 'Spare me the seduction scene, if you don't mind. I'm already aware of your capabilities in that direction and I have no intention of allowing a repeat of what I imagine must have been—on my part, at least—a very amateurish performance!' Even to mention the episode that had haunted her continuously day and night sent claws digging into her heart, but for her own defence she wanted to appear liberated, to wipe out the impression he had formed of a naïve girl so appallingly immature in her approach to sex that she had actually *shed tears*!

Visibly, Tareq controlled an impulse to follow her and across the space dividing he urged with deceptive sincerity. 'I want you for my wife, Lucille, not just now, this minute, but for a lifetime! Why do you fight the inevitable? You know how perfectly we are suited, we could be so happy together, *mon amour*, two halves of a perfect whole. Perhaps you think the rites that bind us are too simple to be believable, nevertheless, I promise you will never be able to disregard them to the extent of entering into marriage with any other man!'

She stared at him, her eyes enormous in a pale, frightened face. What he said was true. She did feel bound, so bound the idea of marriage to any other man seemed sinful, yet she was not prepared to accept a position as doormat in an establishment

162

where Shani reigned supreme. She traced his mouth with her eyes, remembering how intensely he had kissed Shani, how he had quietened her with promises, and how calmly he had agreed to the plans outlined for her own future. Could it be that the ruthless hawk was suffering qualms of conscience? Was he offering marriage as a job for life to compensate for past—and future—treachery?

Complete lack of heat lent finality to her answer. 'I suppose you think I should feel grateful for your offer, *monsieur*, but I do not, I feel insulted! If you were the last man on earth I would not marry you because, knowing you as I do, I would be condemning myself to an existence completely devoid of happiness.'

It was a credit to his tremendous acting ability that he should appear shaken. She did not soften. 'Forget the idea of using marriage to me as a barrier, Shani can be very possessive, but in time you will learn how best to handle her.'

As silence fell between them her nervous fingers plucked silver threads from her skirt, puckering into extinction a heart no less fragile than her own. He took a long time to reply, the interval stretching into infinity as she examined minutely the pattern on her dress, sensing his eyes boring into her face. She had become so used to the silence that when finally his voice broke into the void she was startled. Sounding savagely impatient of defeat, he grated, 'I could bend your will to mine! Here at the oasis an unwilling wife would go unremarked upon, except perhaps to inherit the title of stubborn little mule!'

With a last imprecation he discarded words and grabbed her, pressing his mouth so hard upon hers that she had to clutch his shirt to support her buckling knees. Passion rose high within him as he fought to conquer her with kisses that seared, seeking to prove his dominance over the one woman who would never willingly surrender. Employing all the ploys of an expert, he subjected her to the masterful touches of a maestro aware to the nth degree of the effect of every chord he struck.

Lucille was shaken to the core when with massive effort he curbed rampant desire. Punishing kisses had struck no answering spark, her reaction to his caresses had been a stiffening of every limb so as to combat the treacherous longing of nerves ecstatically responsive to his slightest touch. With an aggravated oath, Tareq ripped the pins from her hair, scattering jewels to the four corners of the room, then grabbing a handful of golden hair he twisted savagely until her head was levered against his chest. '*Tormenteuse!*' he gritted, revelling in her agony, 'you dare to despise me with a child's eyes even while you madden and entice with a seductive body!' She staggered when suddenly he thrust her from him before stalking across to the window, his clenching and unclenching fists betraying a terrible ordeal of control.

Worn out by emotional upheaval, Lucille dragged her body in the direction of the bed, then collapsed with a sob on to its silken surface. A noise like pounding surf was reverberating through her head and her limbs shook as if with fever as reaction took toll of her tortured senses. From across a yawning chasm Tareq's voice reached, grimly controlled.

'You may leave the oasis as soon as you please.

Obviously, there is no point in your remaining now ...'

Her heart soared on slow, laborious wings. 'Thank you ...' she gulped, then lapsed into silence.

He turned to leave, but paused to reflect when he reached the door, startling her with the observation, 'To make love does not necessarily mean to seduce —You asked me what happened between us in the desert and my answer could have been misleading. I made love to you—would probably have seduced you—but unfortunately you fainted ...'

With the sudden *volte-face* of which he was capable he had reverted once more to the rôle of sophisticate. Gone completely was the desert savage who obeyed no demands other than his own and in his place was a suave man of the world who, though impatient of convention, felt obliged to abide by its rules. Lucille choked on a thousand questions; unable to believe that even he could play such a delibately cruel trick. 'You mean you didn't ... I didn't ...?' Words petered out, but grey eyes begged for confirmation.

'No, *we* did not!' he mocked her trembling mouth and shocked eyes with an ease that condemned him as an unprincipled rake.

She groped for a reason, willing him even then to present her with a believable excuse. 'But why?' she whispered. 'What possible benefit could you hope to gain from allowing me to believe ...'

His casual shrug killed every last hope. 'I gambled and lost,' he admitted lightly. 'Deciding when one holds a winning hand is not a matter of choice but of knowledge—an amalgam of "know-how" accumulated over a lifetime of gambling—plus the ability to assess the strength of the opposition. In this case I failed miserably to evaluate correctly, misjudged your ability to resist, possibly even over-estimated my own art of persuasion. Whichever was responsible hardly matters; instead of the reaction I expected you withdrew from me so completely that I'm now beginning to suspect your hatred is the only bond between us. Am I correct, *chérie*?' he prompted so carelessly that she felt her answer barely mattered.

In a quiet way she was capable of fury. She itched to strike her hand across his mocking mouth, but not even that satisfaction would have wiped out the pain and anguish he had caused her. So she strangled the impulse and concentrated her wrath in one succinct sentence.

'*You are totally despicable!*'

Tareq acknowledged the sentiment with a bow, then as his hand reached towards the door he drawled a final question. 'Tell me, for I am curious, exactly why was I rejected? In my book you register as my only failure, but there has to be a reason. Does ambition occupy your full attention? Were it any other woman I would immediately suspect another man, but in your case that can hardly apply.'

Proudly her head rose. 'And why not, pray?' she flashed, hating his patronage.

Dark eyebrows winged with surprise, then drew together. Claw-sharp, he bit out, 'Are you hinting that some other man interests you? That you are in love? *C'est impossible!* With whom ... I can think of no one ...?'

'There's Art,' she rasped, sorely tried.

To her utter surprise he believed her. The blankness of shock deepened his eyes to black as he retreated in silence, his mouth a grim line, his features a bronze, expressionless mask.

CHAPTER FOURTEEN

ART insisted upon accompanying Lucille to the airport. Questions hung between them as they travelled first to Cairo, then, after a late meal at the hotel where they had previously stayed, on to the airport. The shock he had felt at the news of her departure still lingered, even though three days had passed since she had begged his help to arrange her passage home. As they sat together in the departure lounge, his long legs sprawled in front of him, he contemplated with a deep frown a minute scuff on the toecap of his shoe.

Lucille discarded the magazine she had been pretending to read and laid a pleading hand on his arm. 'You're not to worry about me, Art, do you hear?' She countered his moody glance with a smile pinned on to lips that dared not tremble. Then in a tone deliberately light she attempted to tease, 'Surely you weren't taken in by the elaborate pretence played out for the benefit of Tareq's mother? If you think about it, Art,' her lips twisted into a stiff smile, 'you'll realize Tareq could never be seriously interested in me.'

'I have thought about it!' he replied sharply, 'and it seems to me that you and he were admirably suited. Tareq needs someone like you! For so many years he's suffered the attentions of the wrong kind of women, women so bent upon becoming his wife they'd stop at nothing to achieve that end. Then he met you,' he stated simply, as if no further embellishment were needed. 'No matter what you say, I still believe Tareq was the happiest man aboard ship the night he announced your engagement.'

'Don't be ridiculous!' Feeling suddenly breathless, Lucille fumbled in her handbag until she felt composed enough to stress, 'The engagement was manufactured as a protection against Shani—being so strongly attracted to her he felt in need of a shield, so he used me as a preventive against losing his precious freedom!'

Art shook his head. 'That explanation simply doesn't ring true! Tareq is so expert at handling women—I know, because his success has so often amazed me—that I simply can't imagine any situation arising that would render him devoid of tactics. Compared with his ability to escape entanglement Houdini was a mere novice!'

She jumped to her feet, unbearably agitated. His refusal to accept the truth was not helping her departure; she knew that back at the oasis Shani and Tareq would most probably be rehearsing a love scene, infusing more than an element of reality into the production, and it was stupid of Art to imply that she meant anything at all to the man who had let her step out of his life with only the most cursory of goodbyes.

At that precise moment her flight number was called and with tremendous relief she lifted her cheek for his parting kiss. 'Goodbye, Art,' she choked on an onrush of tears, 'thank you so much for your many acts of friendship. I'll treasure them all my life. Don't forget to call on me when you return to London!'

'I certainly won't,' he assured gruffly, tightening

his grip on her shoulders. 'And remember,' he shook her fondly, 'I expect you to enjoy the voyage. I went to a great deal of trouble to arrange it, so repay me by taking advantage of every facility offered on the trip home.'

'I will!' she called across her shoulder as she retreated from the solitary figure who represented the last link with a phase in her life she would have to strive desperately hard to forget.

The pile of papers lying on her desk was the culmination of a year's work. The last chapter had just been completed, and as she surveyed the neatly-typed pages Lucille wondered why she felt disinterest instead of the expected thrill of attainment. She glanced around, wondering, not for the first time, if Art's brainwave was actually a big mistake. 'You deserve a little spoiling,' he had insisted when she had objected to his extravagant gesture of booking the Queen Anne Suite on the *Q.E.*2 for her passage home. 'It seemed so providential,' he had informed her upon his return to the hotel. 'When the booking agent mentioned that the liner had been delayed at Bali I immediately thought—why not? A quick flight, then a few weeks cruising in luxurious surroundings is exactly the tonic you need, plus time to type your last chapter so as to be able to present the finished article to your publisher immediately you reach London!'

It had seemed a good idea at the time. Unfortunately, instead of enabling her to forget, the familiar surroundings had encouraged a rush of memories so painful she had regretted fiercely her weakness in not insisting upon a quick, impersonal flight home. She left the desk and drifted across to gaze out of the huge picture window. Sunbeams were dancing across the waves, casting a mesh of silver over deep blue sea. Inside, no sense of urgency could be felt, but from where she stood the rush of water was evident, and sadly she reflected that each turn of the screws was increasing rapidly the distance between her empty, numbed body and the man who had plundered her heart.

Firm footsteps approaching down the alleyway captured her attention. She held her breath when they halted outside her door, then slowly relaxed when she heard them move on towards the adjacent suite. Several times during her week aboard the same thing had happened, and each time she had expected to hear a knock preceding a forceful, slightly accented voice calling her by name. Of course she was being fanciful. Her stubborn disinclination to leave the suite, even for meals, had its roots in a morbid wish to return to the time when Tareq had occupied the suite next door, instead of this mysterious stranger whose prowlings most likely held no more sinister significance than a desire to be on sociable terms with his nearest neighbour. She gave herself a shake—if she continued much longer with her self-imposed exile she might find the exercise habit-forming! Tonight, she would dress and for the first time since coming aboard would appear in the dining-room for dinner.

By pretending a prearranged meeting with the unknown stranger, Lucille managed to infuse a little enthusiasm into her dressing. She chose a dress Tareq had particularly admired, a filmy, cream-coloured confection, softly feminine, with a swirling skirt, snug-fitting waist and full, diaphanous sleeves caught tightly in at the wrists. She hesitated, her fingers hovering undecidedly over her scant collection of jewellery, then descending as if magnetized upon the golden anklet the Princess had pledged her to keep. She snapped it around her arm, above the elbow, and felt aesthetic pleasure when it glistened through chiffon like moonlight through mist. *'By the wearing of the anklet during the Blessing Ceremony it has become your talisman against evil,'* the Princess had insisted. *'So personal has it become that henceforth it may be worn only by yourself or a descendant, a daughter, perhaps, who has reached marriageable age!'* Even now it hurt unbearably to recall how philosophically the Princess had accepted the news of her departure. She had gone to return the jewellery, expecting to become involved in awkward explanations, only to be confounded by the greeting:

'Ah, *ma petite,* have you come to say goodbye? I was sorry when Tareq told me that you were leaving us, but then I suppose I am a selfish old woman too outmoded in my views to appreciate the importance young women of today place upon a career. You have written a book, I believe,' she had continued casually, dipping gem-encrusted fingers into a dish of fat dates stuffed with pink marzipan.

'Yes ...' Lucille had stammered, taken aback by the unexpected lack of resistance. She had come prepared for reproaches, tears even—anything other than cool indifference.

'You must write to me when you reach England,' the amazing old lady had instructed, paying minute attention to the task of washing sticky fingers in a bowl of water floating with rose petals.

'Of course,' she had agreed faintly, 'but before I go I must apologize ...'

'No need, my dear!' the Princess had beamed. 'Tareq has already explained, I understand perfectly.' Lucille had backed out of her presence, more hurt than she could bear by the offhand dismissal, lingering only long enough to hear the Princess voice a last unexpected request. 'You will remember to wear the amulet always? Keep it about your person, then no harm will befall you ...'

She entered the busy dining-room and was immediately shown to a table adjacent to the marble-framed fountain that was a highlight of the room's exquisite decor. The tinkling of water against stone reminded her of the palace where midday heat was tempered inside large downstair rooms by sculptured forms emitting streams of water from marbled lips on to waterlily cups floating gently on the surface of ancient stone basins. She dragged her mind back from the past to study the menu, wishing she had kept to her usual custom of ordering milk and sandwiches to be served in her suite. Nothing appealed, mouthwatering dishes created by masters of culinary art did nothing to stir the interest of a dulled appetite.

'Just a plain omelette, please,' she instructed the hovering steward, uncomfortably aware of her solitude amidst tables occupied by absorbed people—family parties and sociable passengers who had discovered in the easy, relaxed atmosphere of cruising a new aptitude for making friends. After she had eaten she did not linger. The steward had informed her that a cabaret was about to begin in the Queen's

Room, but even as she had thanked him she had known that some restless inner spirit would not allow her to enjoy the entertainment, so she slipped along to her suite for a wrap, deciding that walking was preferable to being pitched into the midst of an animated throng whose company she did not relish.

She drifted along deserted decks, her slight figure slendered by moonlight to the substance of a wraith, leaning now and then against the ship's rail to admire silvered sea and the night formation of clouds illuminated from behind by a moon gliding through the heavens with a restlessness that underlined her own inner dissatisfaction. With sudden impatience she turned in the direction of light and sound, deciding that any kind of company was preferable to her own, and continued with inner reluctance towards the nearest room likely to offer some form of diversion.

With one foot across the threshold she hesitated; the occupants were all male, their heads bent downwards under clouds of cigar smoke, their eyes riveted upon playing cards palmed within one hand while their free hands coped with a variety of spirit glasses. Dedication was obvious in the silence filling the suede-lined card room and in the rapt concentration of each player trying to assess the strength of his opponent's hand. Lucille's heart gave a tremendous lurch as, just before turning away, her attention was caught by a dark head, arrogantly held, and she hurried out of the room just a split second too late to avoid being noticed by the man who looked up, then, with a few hurried words to his startled companions, pushed back his chair and abandoned the game.

As she flew along deserted alleyways in the direction of her suite, her heart was heavy with despair. If the shape of a dark head, the sight of broad shoulders, were forever to affect her in such a way where in the world was she to find peace? Her headlong rush was halted when she blundered into an obstacle shrouded by gloom. She staggered back, momentarily dazed, and was caught and held in arms that reached her out of the darkness. '*En garde, ma petite*, you will do yourself an injury!'

Lucille spun round, bewildered by a fantasy come to life, but the arms that held her were boldly familiar and the eyes twinkling down full of remembered devilry.

'Tareq!' she breathed as if expectant of his sudden disappearance. 'How...? Why...? I don't understand...'

His easy laughter echoed across the ocean. 'It is a long and complicated story, *mon amie*, so I suggest we seek comfort for the telling. Which would you prefer, your suite—or mine?'

'M ... mine!' she stammered, still confused by his sudden appearance.

'As you wish,' he agreed, a glint denoting amusement at her reluctance to enter his territory. As he escorted her towards the suite he carried on an easy conversation. 'For days I have watched for you, several times I have been on the point of knocking on your door, but then I remembered the importance of your work and bade my soul be patient in the hope that the voyage would not be completely over by the time you appeared.' As they halted at her door he squeezed her hand tightly. 'I'm so glad you decided to appear this evening,' he told her simply. 'I've waited too long.'

Her heart spiralled, the fluttering in her throat threatened to choke. She dared not examine his motives, nor allow her caution to be seduced by the powerful attraction he was projecting. His actions were always motivated by self-interest, she calmed her racing heart, and though she was eager to have the miracle of his presence explained it was with restrained hospitality that she invited him to enter her suite.

It was exquisite agony to watch him lounging in the chair he had previously occupied at Shani's invitation, and pleasurably unnerving to feel his eyes upon her every movement as she served him with a drink and then obeyed his wordless command to share with him the comfort of a deep, velvet-covered settee. Perched nervously on the edge farthest from him, she sipped her drink and pleaded, '*Now*, will you please explain?'

Tareq set his glass down upon a nearby table and with a sleek movement somehow managed to divide the space between them. When Lucille jerked upright, betraying alarm, he relaxed against the cushions and with a smile sought a cheroot case from an inner pocket. 'Have you a light?' he murmured. 'I seem to have mislaid my lighter.'

Flustered, she rose to fetch a table lighter, but when she stooped to set it down within his reach his brown fingers reached out to shackle her wrist, drawing her forward and down until she was imprisoned closely to his side. 'Comfortable?' he queried with a grin. Lucille clenched her fists in her lap, helpless to combat his mastery of a rôle he must have played many times before. Once again he was finding her naïveté entertaining, she decided rebelliously. He was like a gourmet who had suddenly discovered a penchant for plain fare!

Coolly she reminded him, 'We came here to talk, and I'm still waiting for an explanation of your presence aboard ship.'

The quirk that had been playing around his mouth disappeared, leaving behind a grim reminder of the Arab hawk whose beak could wound, then almost immediately he reverted to normal—if his former attitude *was* normal—Lucille was so confused she hardly knew!

'I suppose my reason for being here could be classified as business,' he informed her idly, 'but then again, it might possibly turn out to be pleasure.'

'Whatever your object, it must merit a great deal of importance in your eyes when you've left the film unit high and dry in the middle of production. What was Art's reaction when you told him of your intention to absent yourself at such a critical time?'

Lazily he sized her up, then surprised her by admitting, 'Actually it was he who urged me to come. He became quite agitated, in fact, at the idea of my missing out on what he termed "the most crucial turning point of my life".'

'I see ...' she lied, struggling to think what further peaks remained to be conquered by the man who had already reached such great heights. She lifted her head, perplexed by a thought. 'Then why are you travelling by sea? If your business is so important shouldn't you have gone by air?'

He sprang to his feet, pulling her up beside him, his reckless glint as puzzling as his evasive answer.

'I felt in need of a rest,' he answered succinctly. With disarming charm he began stroking a caressing finger along the curve of her cheek. 'This opportunity might never occur again, *chérie*, so why don't we both take advantage of the voyage to relax, to play together, to have fun with no questions asked and no answers given. What do you think?' he urged in a seducing whisper. 'Are you agreeable?'

His touch awakened dormant nerves; pulses hammered through her body as she stood with bowed head seeking reasons to refuse his amazing suggestion. Endure hours alone in his company! Suffer intimate moments spent dancing, swimming or dining together in a relaxed, carefree atmosphere devoid of outside influences! Would she be mad to accept the offer of a few glorious weeks with the man who, for all his faults, she adored madly, knowing full well the discipline that would have to be brought to bear in order to hide her love from his intuitive eyes? Knowing also that on the horizon would be hovering the heartbreak of a parting even more unbearable than the last? No woman on earth would voluntarily choose to suffer such a fate!

Breathlessly, she told him: 'Very well, if you promise that things will be kept on a strictly friendly basis, then I agree!'

The experiment began the next morning with Tareq assuming an air of friendly companionship more in keeping with the rôle of a man just recently introduced than with that of one who previously had contrived to manoeuvre her into situations much more intimate. As they breakfasted together he steered the conversation along impersonal lines, carefully avoiding any reference to the past, making certain that not the slightest physical contact was made as he plied her with crisp rolls and offerings from the fruit platter. After a while her taut nerves began to relax as gradually his tactics began to succeed. She would not have been human had she not felt gratified by the way in which he choked off would-be intruders, or by the envious glances being cast in her direction by girls infinitely more beautiful and worldly than herself. Tareq reacted caustically when she put her doubts into words. They had left the dining-room and were taking a leisurely stroll around the deck when she felt compelled to assure him.

'If you wish to join your friends please don't hesitate on my account,' she urged with eyes an earnest grey.

He stopped parading to regard her, fresh as dew, in a pink sun-dress with halter neckline leaving her shoulders bare. Her skin scorched under his sliding glance, then a confused sweep of lashes dusted her cheeks when with masterly understatement he commented, 'I prefer to remain with you.' After that Lucille felt no reason to hold her enjoyment in check or to restrain the stream of words that flowed constantly between them as they discussed, argued and generally enjoyed exploring each other's minds. Attraction, they discovered, went far beyond the physical; she blossomed under the new respect he accorded her, never sweeping aside her opinions as the vapourings of a mere woman, but countering seriously when he disagreed and delving fully and intently into the many subjects in which they found themselves in complete accord. Days and nights ran into a week, the most wonderful week Lucille had ever lived—a dream from which she never wanted to awake lest awakening should bring forgetfulness.

They were lazing on the sun deck when, after a further spirited discussion, Tareq settled back in his chair with the observation, 'With you, *chérie*, each day brings fresh delight. Most of the women I've known would expect every hour to be devoted to flattery—the endless pursuit of the female by the male—but you have the gift of enabling a man to treat you as an equal while at the same time retaining every iota of femininity.'

'Careful!' she teased, now happily relaxed in his company. 'Wasn't it Sophocles who said: "Once a woman is made equal to man she becomes his superior"?'

He lunged forward, threatening retribution, and with a laugh she tried to dodge away. But he was too quick for her; she was trapped by the wrist, so close he was a mere breath away. For seconds their laughing eyes clung, then silence fell, a silence into which battened-down emotions escaped to make riotous mockery of good intentions. Instinctively, Lucille's tender young mouth lifted when he lowered his head. She closed her eyes, anticipating the furore of his kiss, then became aware of a battle within him that culminated in the grip upon her arm becoming agonizing. With cruel lack of warning she was released and coldly ordered, 'We must go! As we are expected to appear at the captain's cocktail party this evening you'll need plenty of time to change.'

She reacted as if struck. Struggling with mortified tears, she managed a constricted whisper. 'I suppose you're right—no, please don't come with me!' she panicked when he stood up to accompany her. 'I'll see you later . . .'

She had ample time to reflect before dressing for dinner. Once inside her suite she threw herself upon the settee and drew up her knees until she was a tightly curled ball of misery full of tears aching to be shed. Why, oh, *why* had she allowed herself to spoil a wonderful relationship? She, who had had to be convinced Tareq had meant it when he spoke of keeping feelings platonic, had been the very one to break faith! She moaned, recognizing her inability to love merely with the mind. Friendship with Tareq could never be enough—*more than anything in the world she wanted his love*!

From somewhere, that evening, Lucille drew forth a new air of dignity. Perhaps her dress helped—a black sheath hitherto in disfavour because its impact of sophistication jarred violently with her natural demureness—or it might have been her eyes, mirroring courage, or an inherited breeding that decreed that humiliation must be borne with patrician head held high. Whichever was responsible, she drew strength from the knowledge that she looked far from downcast when she answered Tareq's knock upon her door.

'No, I won't come in,' he refused tightly when she stepped back to admit him. 'We haven't much time, so if you're quite ready we'll go straight along to the captain's cabin.'

'Just as you wish,' she replied, wondering if he, too, was shocked by the ice tinkling in her voice. She was never to know. Silently he helped her on with her wrap, treating her creamy shoulders as if they represented scorching danger to unwary fingers, then led her along the alleyways to the lift, his eyes stern, his athletic, elegantly clad body disciplined and erect.

Many times during the following hour Lucille yearned to ask him if he would prefer to leave, yet perversely, because he was obviously in no mood to enjoy trivial conversation, he lingered until dinner chimes sounded, prolonging his conversation with a senior officer until the unfortunate man had no option but to plead pressing duties in order to escape. It was not until that moment that realization struck: she had embarrassed him so much he no longer wished to be alone with her! Whip-sharp, the knowledge stung. Swallowing utter degradation she shot out the staccatoed words!

'I—I shan't be dining with you after all ... not hungry ... please excuse me ...'

Blindly she sped the length of deserted decks, the length of her stride hampered by a slim sheath of skirt, stumbling in slender-heeled sandals fashioned for purposes purely decorative. But her ravaged mind, occupied with the desire to escape, registered neither discomfort nor warning of the folly of rushing headlong into unlit space, so when eventually she careered into the back of a parading officer the impact caught her completely unawares.

'Good lord!' Hands reached out to steady her when shock buckled her knees. 'Are you hurt? I'm terribly sorry, I had no idea you were behind me!'

'Thank you, officer, I'll take care of her.' Tareq's breathing was harsh as he loomed out of the darkness to take complete charge. She had no strength left to fight, so meekly she allowed him to direct her towards the boat deck where the solitude and silence were frightening. Vaguely, she registered that he had chosen for their showdown the exact spot in which he had forced her to accept his proposal, and the memory of all the pain and humiliation she had since suffered inflicted further strain upon her lacerated feelings.

His first words sounded like a condemnation. 'My plan did not work out, did it? But then I must confess I never really expected that it would. Platonic friendship can exist between a man and a woman only if neither is attracted—which is why the idea was doomed from the very beginning ...'

Lucille hated the cold, emotionless way he set out his argument, dragging out the words from between lips uncompromisingly stern. Like a battered flower set to defy further storm, her head lifted, her grey eyes seeking his in the brooding darkness. She was close enough to distinguish his hawk-sharp features, but did not stop to wonder why his expressionless mask should betray such a surprising lack of triumph. All she wanted was peace, and defeat echoed in her listless answer.

'I'm sorry, Tareq, if I have embarrassed you, I tried to hide my love for you, but obviously I didn't succeed ...'

She faltered at the sound of a harsh, indrawn breath. He was mere inches away, so immobile he might have been carved from stone. Remaining rigidly still, he hissed, *'What did you say?'*

Lucille recoiled from a dam of emotion surging to burst its bonds. 'I promise not to become a nuisance,' she sobbed. 'Once we leave the ship you'll never see me again——'

It could have been a tidal wave that lifted her from her feet, so effortlessly, so swiftly and so fiercely was she swept up into his arms. Her bitter tears mingled with his passionate words of adoration as with unleashed ferocity he pleaded, chided and punished her with kisses that began as a storm and continued until she was a sweet, confused bundle of disbelief weathering the poignant delight of a holocaust. '*Mon amour*!' he murmured fiercely against the pink shell of her ear. '*Je t'adore.*' As his lips progressed along the gentle curve of her cheek, feathered against thick golden lashes, plundered her quivering mouth, stroked with possessive fervour against her throat and the tender innocence of a bared shoulder, Lucille began to believe the wild promises contained in words thick with passion. '*My darling*!' he had said, over and over again. '*I adore you!*'

She was a storm-tossed piece of jetsam clinging helplessly to his strength by the time he was ready to curb his tempestuous impulses. Allowing her respite, Tareq cradled her slimness in his arms and with his cheek resting upon hair of tousled gold he berated softly, 'How I curse the English reserve that enabled you to hide from me the love I yearned! Have you any idea, I wonder, what fiendish torture your cool disdain inflicted? Of the many times I hoped, despaired, then dared to hope again, only to be cast down once more to bottomless depths?' His voice shook as once more he demanded: 'Tell me again, repeat slowly those wonderful words that released me from my hell!'

Lucille stirred, bemused with happiness, but still unsure enough to question, 'How can you possibly love me? What about Shani...?'

'*Say it*!' he demanded, imperious in desire. With touching sincerity she obeyed, as she knew she was fated always to obey. 'I love you, my wild hawk, I will love you even beyond eternity!' They exchanged a kiss more binding than vows, full of sweetness and contentment, almost passionless but treasured for its depth of commitment. With lips softly clinging, she reproached him, 'Why didn't you say you loved me at the beginning instead of concocting such an elaborate pretence?'

'You wouldn't have believed me,' he answered simply. 'Anyway, the idea of yourself being used as my protection against Shani's supposedly deadly charms was yours. I merely pretended to agree.'

'Mine?'

'Yes, *mon coeur*,' he teased. 'My plan was to use Shani to make you jealous, and I thought I had succeeded,' he admitted, 'the night you watched me kissing her. I saw your reflection in a mirror—I thought I had acted most convincingly, too convincingly as it turned out, because afterwards you became even more unapproachable.'

'Are you admitting,' she accused him indignantly, 'that you manipulated both Shani and myself to further your own ends?'

'*Chérie*,' he whispered with rising passion, 'I would have gone to far greater lengths!'

'Fiend!' she adored him. 'Your mother would be appalled to hear you say so!'

'Ah, yes, Maman!' he grinned. 'The wise old owl was correct in her assumption that all that was needed was an interval alone together without disturbing influences: "You must learn to be friends

185

before you can become lovers," ' she assured me. 'At the time my impatience fought with her wisdom, but her words have been proved correct. We are friends, are we not, *ma petite adorée*,' he seduced her with a whisper, 'therefore there is no reason why we should not soon become lovers . . .'

Willingly Lucille raised her lips, revelling in a happiness almost too great to be borne. 'I want so much to be your wife, Tareq, to cook for you, to wait on you, to bring your slippers . . .'

He smothered a laugh, loving her look of earnestness, but prompted by the memory of her spirited views of the emancipation of women, he asked, 'And what will you expect from me in return, beloved?'

She snuggled closer. 'I shall expect to become one of the adored, cosseted women behind the veil,' she sighed her contentment. Thrilled by his dominance, enraptured by his touch, yet awesomely aware that the heart beating vigorously beneath her hand would respond only to her—the desert hawk, unbroken in spirit, wild of wing, had found its resting place and was deeply content.

Mills & Boon
Best Seller Romances

Mills & Boon Best Seller Romances

The very best of Mills & Boon Romances
brought back for those of you who missed
them when they were first published.

In March
we bring back the following four
great romantic titles.

DANGEROUS RHAPSODY
by Anne Mather

Emma's job in the Bahamas was not as glamorous as it seemed
– for her employer, Damon Thorne, had known her before –
and as time went on she realised that he was bent on using her
to satisfy some strange and incomprehensible desire for
vengeance . . .

THE NOBLE SAVAGE
by Violet Winspear

The rich, appallingly snobbish Mrs Amy du Mont would have
given almost anything to be admitted to the society of the
imposing Conde Estuardo Santigardas de Reyes. But it was
Mrs du Mont's quiet, shy little companion who interested the
Conde . . .

TEMPORARY WIFE
by Roberta Leigh

Luke Adams was in love with his boss's wife, and it was
essential that their secret should remain a secret — so Luke
made a temporary marriage of convenience with Emily Lamb.
But Emily didn't know Luke's real reason for marrying her . . .

MASTER OF THE HOUSE
by Lilian Peake

Alaric Stoddart was an arrogant and autocratic man, who had
little time for women except as playthings. 'All women are the
same,' he told Petra. 'They're after two things and two things
only — money and marriage, in that order.' Could Petra prove
him wrong?

If you have difficulty in obtaining any of these books through
your local paperback retailer, write to:

Mills & Boon Reader Service
P.O. Box 236, Thornton Road, Croydon, Surrey, CR9 3RU.

A new idea in romance for Mothers Day

Mothers Day is Sunday March 29th. This year, for the first time ever, there's a special Mills & Boon Mothers Day Gift Pack.* Best Seller Romances by favourite authors are presented in this attractive gift pack. The pack costs no more than if you buy the four romances individually.

It is a lovely gift idea for Mothers Day. Every mother enjoys romance in reading.

DANGEROUS MASQUERADE
Janet Dailey

TO BUY A BRIDE
Roberta Leigh

BEWARE THE BEAST
Anne Mather

THE CHILD OF JUDAS
Violet Winspear

*Available in UK from Feb. 13th

£3.00

The rose of romance
Mills & Boon

Masquerade
Historical Romances

Intrigue
excitement
romance

LADY OF STARLIGHT
by Margot Holland

Gilbert de Boveney saved Lady Alyce de Beaumont
from the lust of a neighbouring Count, but it was his
twin brother she longed to marry. Or was it?

CAMILLA
by Sara Orwig

Camilla Hyde's only hope of escaping from the British
troops devastating Washington in 1814 lay with Jared
Kingston. He had made it clear that he was not
interested in her, but she would have travelled with the
Devil himself to get home to England!

Look out for these titles in your local paperback shop from
13th February 1981

The Mills & Boon Rose is the Rose of Romance

Every month there are ten new titles to choose from — ten new stories about people falling in love, people you want to read about, people in exciting, far-away places. Choose Mills & Boon. It's your way of relaxing:

February's titles are:

TEMPLE OF FIRE by *Margaret Way*
Julian Stanford had everything except a heart. Could Fleur possibly stand up to him and his overwhelming family?

ONE BRIEF SWEET HOUR by *Jane Arbor*
If Dale Ransome still chose to think the worst of Lauren, let him. She just didn't care any more — did she?

WHEN MAY FOLLOWS by *Betty Neels*
Had Katrina been incredibly foolish to want to change her life by marrying Professor Raf van Tellerinck?

LIVING TOGETHER by *Carole Mortimer*
The attractive Leon Masters was determined to get through the ice that enclosed Helen — but was his method the right one?

SEDUCTION by *Charlotte Lamb*
Clea wasn't too enthusiastic about her arranged marriage to Ben Winter, until he came along to turn her feelings upside down . . .

A GIRL POSSESSED by *Violet Winspear*
Was Janie a good enough actress to conceal her love for Pagan Pentrevah, and pretend to be married to him to keep his ex-wife at bay?

THE SUGAR DRAGON by *Victoria Gordon*
The forceful Con Bradley was quite enough for Verna to cope with, even before Madeline Cunningham arrived, with wedding bells in mind!

NEVER COUNT TOMORROW by *Daphne Clair*
Lin fell in love with Soren Wingard and everything crashed about her in ruins. Could she get away from him before she did any more harm?

ICEBERG by *Robyn Donald*
What heart Justin Doyle had belonged to his dead wife Alison. Hadn't Linnet better leave Justin to her sister Bronwyn?

AN ISLAND LOVING by *Jan MacLean*
All Kristin knew was that he brought her more happiness — and bitter unhappiness — than she had ever known. Would she ever be free of him again?

If you have difficulty in obtaining any of these books from your local paperback retailer, write to:

Mills & Boon Reader Service
P.O. Box 236, Thornton Road, Croydon, Surrey, CR9 3RU.